MARK ONE:
THE DUMMY

MARK ONE: THE DUMMY

John Ball

Little, Brown and Company — Boston – Toronto

FIRST EDITION

T 09/74

LIBRARY OF CONGRESS CATALOGING IN PUBLICATION DATA

Ball, John Dudley, 1911-
    Mark one - the dummy.

    I. Title.
PZ4.B187Mar   [PS3552.A455]   813 .5'4   74-7365
ISBN 0-316-07950-2

*Published simultaneously in Canada
by Little, Brown & Company (Canada) Limited*

PRINTED IN THE UNITED STATES OF AMERICA

For Martin Bury

Author's Note

Very sincere thanks are due, and are tendered here, to the many persons who have generously consented to appear in this book. Their unstinting help and advice have been quite literally invaluable.

May I acknowledge also the contributions by many institutions and organizations, such as Ullstein Verlag of Berlin, which have made the telling of this story possible.

Two great teachers of the martial arts have extended help and guidance over a period of years: Master Hidetaka Nishiyama, who is probably the foremost karate ka in the world, and the late Master Isao Takahashi, who was the outstanding exponent of aikido in the western hemisphere.

Particular thanks are due to Mr. Jean Ruegg of Escotours, Inc., whose expertise on all matters concerning Europe and the Near East is awesome.

Lastly, before any possible rumors arise, it may be well to add that this work is not autobiographical in any way.

JOHN BALL

MARK ONE:
THE DUMMY

1

THE LOBBY CLOCK behind the desk of the Schweitzerhof Hotel was reaching upward toward ten as an elevator door slid open to release a single passenger coming down from a top-floor suite. The guest had not asked for that type of accommodation, but with a keen eye for sound publicity values the management had provided the upgrade at no increase in rate. As the recipient of this favor came in view of the desk, the ever-alert concierge noted his presence immediately.

"Good morning, Mr. Nesbitt," he greeted him in excellent English. "I hope you had a comfortable night."

The concierge was well aware that the guest was on his way to a press conference, hence the very gentle hint that

3

a mention of the hotel at an appropriate moment would be in order.

"Good morning, Herr Gombert. I rested very well — and again my thanks to the manager for the flowers and the fruit."

"Entirely our pleasure, sir. Have a nice day."

The man called Nesbitt paused for a moment and then walked out onto the Budapester Strasse where he was greeted by a soothing wash of warm spring air. In late April Berlin was lovely — at least the western half was. Nesbitt had been through Checkpoint Charley the previous day and had taken the well-oiled tour to which his American passport had entitled him. During his short visit to the communist part he had detected nothing of moment, but he had managed to catch a few expressions when people had looked at him, he had noted some scraps in a litter basket, and had cataloged in his well-developed memory the merchandise on display at a news kiosk. He had returned with the feeling that the eastern section of the city was the world's largest penitentiary; the Wall had fixed that idea in his mind with hammering realism. For a few seconds the depressing mood of that visit returned; then he switched his mind back to where he was now.

He accepted the taxi that the doorman had waiting, climbed inside, and said, "Springer Building."

The doorman bent over and repeated the instructions in German. The driver nodded and the Mercedes cab pulled away from the curb. In less than a minute Nesbitt was crossing the busy Kurfürstendamm; as soon as he had done so he glanced at his watch and once more assured himself that he was on time. Some people showed up late for press conferences — he was not one of them. He was very seldom late for anything.

As the taxi rolled on he noted once again how quiet and orderly Berlin was — at least at that hour of the morning. Much of the architecture was early Marlene Dietrich, but apart from that fact the city had about it an almost mid-western American air. There were many trees and the pavement was in uniformly good repair. Nesbitt was very much aware that it was all an island well behind the Iron Curtain, but there was no visible evidence of political realities in the warming morning sunshine.

In less than ten minutes the cab drew up before the considerable plaza that set off the towering Springer Building. Nesbitt got out, paid the fare, and made his way without hurrying toward the principal entrance. He was just inside when he was approached by a lively and attractive German matron still on the right side of middle age. "Mr. Nesbitt, welcome to Berlin! We are so happy to have you here; you know, of course, that you are one of our *most* popular authors. I am Liselotte Kiwit, with the press and public relations section."

"How do you do," Nesbitt said.

"I am so glad that you come a little early for your press conference. It will be on the top floor; please come this way."

With brisk efficiency she led him to the elevators and pressed a button. "Can you speak German? No matter, the press people who will be here all know English. It is fast becoming the universal language, even though no one can learn to spell it."

That sufficed until they had ridden up together; then

5

Nesbitt allowed his hostess to lead the way. After a short corridor he found himself in a very large room that commanded a spectacular view in two opposite directions. Close below on one side was the Wall and immediately behind it the stark Zone of Death with its visible concrete and steel traps and invisible buried mines. He saw it and then tried to block it out of his mind; it was there but he could not accept it — it was inhuman savagery made real and as such it repelled him.

He did not have time to think about it any more as he was led over to where three gentlemen of the publishing firm were on their feet to meet him. Once again the image of midwestern America came to him as he was formally introduced and then with proper protocol offered a drink from the bar. He gave his order to an attentive waiter who had materialized on cue at his side and then made the little speech that was expected of him.

"I want to tell you that I'm most happy to have Ullstein Verlag as my German publishers," he said. "A great many people who read your language much better than I do tell me that your translations are excellent. Also I'm most grateful for the very good sales that you've developed for my books."

The executive on his right responded in English with little accent. "I agree, the sales have been outstanding, but that is entirely because your work is so very good. It is not by accident that Mark Day is tremendously popular all over the world."

During the next few minutes Nesbitt enjoyed himself talking with the three executives about some of the realities of the publishing business. He listened to them carefully and weighed with some care an idea for a possible future book that they laid before him. There was no language barrier and no cultural frontier; they were united in the activity of creating and producing books and that provided a firm common bond. They got along together so well that Nesbitt felt a twinge of regret when Frau Kiwit rejoined the party with a comfortable stack of books tucked under her arm, certain to be copies of the latest Edwin Nesbitt novel to be released in the Ullstein edition.

"Everything is ready," she announced, "and the press people are here."

Nesbitt got to his feet, shook hands once more with his new friends, and then allowed himself to be led across the room to where four more persons, all of them reasonably young, awaited his presence. He always felt self-conscious at moments like that, when he had to greet representatives of various publications he had probably never seen and whose names were unfamiliar. Without any background knowledge to draw on, it would be too easy to make some tactless remark without ever knowing it. He was careful to listen to the names as he was introduced and tried his best to remember them. As soon as he had shaken hands all around he sat down, rested his hands on the arms of his chair, and waited for the inevitable questions concerning the famous character he had created, his methods of working, and himself.

A female with very long, very straight hair and a body to match started things off. "Mr. Nesbitt, *Playboy* magazine said last month that Mark Day is so realistic because a great part of him is really yourself. Is this the truth?"

"I'm very sorry, but I'm afraid that it isn't," Nesbitt

7

replied. "For example: I'm forty-three years old and I stand five feet nine. Mark is in his middle thirties and he is six feet even. He seldom if ever loses his temper; I can't say the same thing."

He paused to let that much sink in.

"Furthermore," he continued. "Day is a highly qualified agent, while I'm simply an author — and you can see what a tremendous difference exists there."

"Perhaps not as much as you say." A male reporter with oversized glasses studied him. "We have all read your books about Mark Day and agree that he is the most believable character in the field. He uses his head when many of his fictional colleagues often do not. And he's ingenious. But that could also describe you; you have to be very ingenious to create the situations that Day encounters, and his solutions to them. Day's devices are your devices. And if I may say so, you do not impress me as any less unflappable than he is."

"You don't know me very well," Nesbitt retorted. "By the way, were you educated in England?"

"Yes, is it my accent in English?"

"Partly, but mostly 'unflappable' is a British term."

The reporter nodded briskly. "See — you prove my point."

A second female in the group, whose generous breasts were on at least partial display, continued the subject. "Mark Day has a thorough knowledge of karate and aikido; much has been said about how accurate you are when you describe his fights. It is that you have studied these arts yourself — is it not so?"

Nesbitt crossed his legs and took a moment or two before he answered that. "I try always to be as accurate as I can,"

8

he said. "For that reason I have studied these arts — yes, and I enjoy them. It is also good exercise and I need that."

He turned back toward the young man with the glasses. "You spoke about Mr. Day's resourcefulness. I hope that he does well, but remember that I have all the time that I need to think out things that he must decide in seconds."

The fourth reporter, a somewhat older male, was ready to make a point. "Look at it this way: yourself and Herr Day are both men and the years which make you apart are perhaps eight at the most. You are also both Americans. So is it not true that you discover much of Herr Day in yourself? How can you avoid it?"

"Because I'm not a secret agent for one thing," Nesbitt answered. "I could never become one. My job is to sit at a typewriter much of the time, and also to do mundane things like trying to keep my budget in balance."

For a moment he stopped, blocking out those who were around him. Then he started over again, but this time he chose his words very carefully. "I am not Mark Day, I want that definitely understood. But also I don't want him ever to become a cardboard character, without any depth or individuality. You have said that he is believable; I put a great deal of effort into trying to make him just that. So when I am writing about him, I sometimes try to project myself into the situation that confronts him. But not in my own person; rather, I try my best to step into his shoes and his character — do you understand what I mean?"

The long-haired girl nodded acceptance. "Like an actor playing a role, something perhaps very different from his own self."

"Yes, that's it! I don't claim to be an actor, but I can visualize better that way — I can sense his emotions and

9

reactions. Then, when I have things worked out, I come back to earth again and try to get my thoughts down on paper."

Apparently that satisfied them, because he could feel their interest ebb in that subject. The female with the unavoidable bosom jiggled herself a little and asked, "Is Mark Day ever going to marry Miss Van Damm?"

Nesbitt relaxed at that and allowed himself to smile. "He may, but that's pretty much up to them."

He answered a few more routine questions about his working methods, and then faced the inevitable political queries which always come up in European press conferences.

"I really don't have any personal politics," he said. "I pretty much tend to mind my own business and try to get my work done."

"But how can you ignore such matters when Mark Day is always involved in international affairs of that kind?" The straight-haired girl was becoming a little irritating.

Nesbitt brushed that aside. "I have my own private preferences, of course. I'm in favor of my own country, and, like Kennedy, I'm for Berlin too. I'd like to see that Wall come down because I don't like tyranny against any people. But I don't get involved in active politics because my work lies elsewhere — is that clear enough?"

The older male reporter came to his rescue with an obvious change of subject. "Is there a real Celestine Van Damm?" he asked.

With gratitude he gave his stock answer. "Miss Van Damm is an internationally minded young woman who belongs to what is commonly called the jet set. However, she isn't empty-headed and very few ordinary men, such as myself, would interest her. Her family is in the diamond business, but her own interests are in archeology and she is entirely serious about it; she has a master's degree in the field. She and Mark Day are good friends and see each other whenever they happen to be in the same area. As to whether or not she is real, let me put it this way: I would know her if I saw her."

At that point Frau Kiwit came to his rescue. "Mr. Nesbitt has to meet other appointments," she announced. "I hope you have enjoyed your visit with him."

The four reporters arose, said the appropriate things, and started off together. As soon as they had gone a few feet away they switched at once into German as they discussed the interview.

Frau Kiwit waited until they were gone. "I think that it was very successful," she said. "I know them very well and they were impressed. They do not sometimes act that way, it is their manner, you understand, but they will write very well about you. One more thing: we would appreciate it if you would autograph a few books for us before you go. . . ."

As soon as that chore had been completed Nesbitt was a free man once more. As he walked back to the elevators he noted for the second time a series of open narrow cages that moved in a continuous loop next to the shafts.

"That is the pater noster," Frau Kiwit explained. "To go up or down a floor or two you just step on and off. It is very handy."

"American insurance companies would be horrified," Nesbitt said. He stood in front of the continuously moving vertical conveyor for a few seconds, gauging the timing, then without difficulty he stepped into one of the narrow cages as it descended and rode it all of the way down to the lobby. As he had anticipated, his hostess came down in the compartment that had been immediately above his own. "Did you like it?" she asked when she had dismounted and was once more beside him.

"It's a good idea," Nesbitt told her, "though our lawyers would probably have fits."

He continued to watch the contraption for several more seconds. "You could stage a very good spy chase in that thing," he added. "What happens if you don't get off at the last floor?"

"You just go around and come up the other side; it is quite safe."

Nesbitt considered that. "I may do something with it," he said.

Five minutes later he was in a taxi that had been provided for him and on his way back to the Schweitzerhof. He felt a certain relief that the press conference, which had been the main reason for his visit to the city, was behind him and that his call at his publishers was also completed. With these things attended to he had almost a full day at his disposal, leaving him free to wander about the city. After all, Berlin was one of the world capitals of intrigue; he was sure he could find some additional inspiration here for the type of fiction in which he specialized.

He checked his watch and decided to have lunch at the hotel. Following that he would engage a car for the afternoon, one with an English-speaking driver qualified to show him places that would be of particular interest in connection with his work. Herr Gombert, the concierge, would arrange it — he seemed to be a man who knew no limitations.

When the taxi had pulled up, he paid the fare with a sense of emancipation. When he was at home, the typewriter was always waiting and there were invariably people to see. In Berlin he knew no one outside of the hotel and the Springer Building. He had no duty calls to pay and there was no way he could be compelled to revise his latest manuscript which, in his opinion, required no revision whatsoever. He crossed the lobby a free man and made his wishes known to Herr Gombert. The concierge understood at once; he promised to have a suitable car with the right driver standing by at thirteen hundred.

More than satisfied, Nesbitt entered the elevator, punched the top button, and ascended. He had had no particular thought in his mind as he started up, but his inventive facilities would not be still; the realization that he was at the very hub of so much international drama triggered him, and a scene flashed into his mind. It would begin in a hotel corridor: suspecting something, Mark Day would slip his key into the lock of his room and open the door noiselessly. That is, he would do it if it was possible. Nesbitt was not sure about that.

The elevator door opened and the carpeted corridor lay before him. No other person was in view, which set the stage for a little experiment if he chose to conduct it.

He walked out of the elevator and started toward his room, slowly and as quietly as he was able. Even though his hearing was excellent, he could not detect that he was making any sound whatever and the floor beneath his feet showed no distressing tendency to creak.

Still unobserved, he reached the door of his suite, his key now in his hand. Bending over, he inserted it into the lock, using the fingers of his left hand to guide it and avoid any scraping of metal on metal. There was a very slight sound as the tumblers were moved, but the thickness of the door was undoubtedly enough to kill it unless the lock transmitted it to the other side. Even then it was so faint it could not be heard, in all probability, more than five feet away.

With exquisite care he pulled the knob slightly toward himself to reduce the friction, and then began to turn it to the right very slowly. To lessen the possibility of a physical slip on his part, he held his breath as he did so.

In a matter of three more seconds the latch cleared the edge of the plate and the door was free. Unable to resist the dramatic effect, even though it was for his benefit alone, he swung the door open swiftly and stepped inside.

The man who was bent over going through his opened suitcase looked up in sudden, startled surprise.

2

WITH THE EYES of a professional observer, Nesbitt cataloged him in one swift glance: age thirty plus, build slender, face seamed, eyes dark, hair black and already thinning, height about five feet eleven, weight close to one seventy. Clothing dark and nondescript, which made him exactly the sort of man whom Mark Day had encountered many times and had always been able to handle one way or another. As that potent thought raced through Nesbitt's brain the intruder whirled to face him, his hands half-open and slightly extended. In one more second he would have his surprise conquered and the initiative back into his hands. A cold shock of danger ran through Nesbitt; although no weapon had appeared, he was suddenly acutely aware that he had none of his own. At that moment he had desperate need of Mark Day, his own creation, who was the man best equipped to deal with this situation, and with that realization his inventive brain snapped into action.

In total command of himself, his sculptured features betraying nothing, Mark Day spoke in his normal voice. "I don't recall having invited you here."

The intruder knew there was no other way out of the suite unless he chose to plunge through a window and meet certain death more than ten stories below. In the second or two of time that he had been given, his quick eyes searched the six-foot figure before him for the betraying bulge of a gun, but the perfectly cut suit that Day wore told him nothing.

With a quick intake the man filled his lungs with air; as he did so a knife flashed into his hand. Cutting edge up, it was lethal and the speed with which it had been produced left no doubt as to the expertness of the man who held it. He was a panther and if he knew who Mark Day was, he showed no indication of either respect or fear.

Still Day did not move, waiting for his opponent to show his hand. The man was perfectly balanced as he stood, but he could not remain that way indefinitely — as soon as he moved he would be at less of an advantage and Day knew it. It was far from a standoff, because every passing moment increased the chances that someone would happen by and see through the open doorway what was taking place.

The man with the knife suddenly lunged forward, but an eyelid had flicked first and Day was ready. With fo-

16

cused power he snapped his left arm up in a rising forearm block as he too sprang forward — something the intruder had not expected.

With catlike speed the man spun his body sideways to the right, but Mark had anticipated him. With his rigid vertical forearm he hit just below the attacker's right elbow, making the knife useless for the better part of a second. As their bodies collided Day dropped and thrust his right shoulder under the intruder's armpit. With practiced skill he first straightened his knees, lifting the man off his feet, then he bent swiftly forward, his two hands holding his opponent's right wrist.

In deadly silence Mark whirled the man over his head with increasing speed and slammed him with concentrated power onto the floor. Despite the thick carpeting the intruder landed flat on his back with stunning force, the knife flying from his uncontrolled fingers. Frantically he attempted to reach for it; as he did so Mark lifted his left leg and with carefully calculated power drove the heel of his foot into the soft part of his opponent's abdomen.

As the air was forced out of his body the man made his first audible sound — an animal cry of pain and defeat. Mark ignored it; he knew that this type of man would have used his knife mercilessly if he had been given the chance, and what he would have done would not have been pleasant. Mark stood ready and waiting, but the man on the floor rolled up his eyeballs and yielded to unconsciousness.

A human body, living or dead, is not an easy thing to dispose of, but Mark had met that situation before — in both of its forms. His mind icy calm, he first kicked the knife out of the way. That done, he stooped over and with-

out undue effort picked up the awkwardly limp form of his late attacker and maneuvered it across his shoulders into a fireman's carry. Then, as calmly as though he were walking down a church aisle, he exited from his suite and started down the corridor in the opposite direction from the one he usually took. He did not plan what he would say if he met anyone — if he did he would think of something to fit the circumstances.

Luck was with him; he reached the end unobserved and there found what he was looking for — the service elevator that common sense and experience had told him would be there. He pressed the button and waited.

A long fifteen seconds later the car leveled off and the door slid open; the elevator was empty. Without ceremony Mark deposited his burden on the floor; then using the knuckle of his forefinger he pushed the button for the basement. As the door closed he stepped outside and then, still apparently entirely relaxed, walked back to his suite. Once again there was no one to observe him and perhaps recall having seen him later on. He stepped back inside his temporary quarters and calmly shut the door behind him.

Once he was safely inside, Edwin Nesbitt leaned his back against the door he had just closed and opened his mouth, the better to pump air into his lungs. His legs were shaking and he knew that he was far from master of himself. His first thought was to ease his tension with a drink; then he remembered that he did not have the necessary ingredients at hand. He could go downstairs and get one, but at that moment public scrutiny was the last thing he desired.

He did not know how he had done it. Of course he had

practiced the common over-the-shoulder throw hundreds of times on the mat, but he had always been conscious of what he was doing. This time he had acted purely mechanically, but the results had been much more spectacular than he had ever attained before. And carrying that limp man down the corridor — what if someone had seen him? He banished that thought from his mind — by the grace of God no one *had* seen him, at least as far as he knew, and somehow he had found the physical strength to carry out that almost gruesome task.

By now someone would have found the man, or he would have found himself. Ed Nesbitt very much doubted that when he came to he would choose to identify the person who was responsible for his condition — he might be more concerned with explaining his presence in the hotel in the first place. Unless he happened to be a guest, of course, and that was quite possible; the easiest way to get into a well-guarded hotel's residential floors was simply to register and go up with a piece of luggage.

He took out his handkerchief and carefully wiped his forehead and his neck. As he did so the thought came to him that despite his sense of recent exertion he had imagined the whole thing. There were such mental illnesses, and he was not necessarily immune. He solved that by stooping down and looking to see if the knife was still where he had kicked it. It was, motionless and still deadly with its shining blade that had to be razor-sharp. The sight of it sickened him and the thought of some cold water came to him. He supplied himself with a glassful in the bathroom and then studied himself in the mirror.

He looked quite the same as he always had — at least in recent years. There were no telltale indications that he could see of what he had just done. Furthermore, every minute that passed without the phone ringing or a tap on his door helped to separate him from the deed he had somehow managed to accomplish. If there was a thorough investigation by the German police, then of course he would be questioned along with everyone else. He debated what he ought to do then and arrived at the highly sensible conclusion that he would quite candidly tell the whole thing. The knife was his proof, that is if it bore a satisfactory set of the intruder's fingerprints. Taking a fresh handkerchief from his recently searched suitcase, he unfolded it and then, picking up the knife by the blade, he carefully wrapped it and slid it into the side of his bag.

When he was done with that he felt much calmer. Checking his appearance once more for any betraying evidence and finding none, he left his suite, went down the corridor the proper way this time, and took an elevator to the lobby. It was time for lunch and the most rational thing that he could think of to do was to go and eat.

He enjoyed his meal in calm solitude; no inquisitors came to ask him to accompany them, and the lentil soup was unexpectedly delicious. When he had finished, he checked with the concierge and found that his car was ready and waiting. The driver had once taken James Michener around the city, or so he said, and he knew who Mark Day was — he had read three of Nesbitt's books in the Ullstein German language editions. He was enthusiastically ready to show Day's creator all of the important places in Berlin that had figured in the western half of the city's lurid past.

Nesbitt reclaimed his attaché case that he had left at the desk and set out to see more of the city that held so many secrets — including one he was keeping himself. As he climbed into the back seat of the Mercedes he tried to comfort himself with the thought that he had interrupted nothing more than a hotel sneak thief, a loner who had no sinister organization behind him likely to track down a hapless American out on a sightseeing tour. He opened his attaché case, took out a block of legal-sized, ruled yellow paper, and prepared to take notes.

His driver took him from one gray monolithic building to another, explaining in each case what had happened behind the massive Teutonic walls that looked as though they could outlast the pyramids. Nesbitt filled several pages of paper with terse notes. With rare intelligence the driver refrained from giving him all of the usual tourist explanations in which he sensed his client was not interested.

When the tour was over Nesbitt checked his case once more at the hotel desk and then set out on foot. He visited the Kaiserkirche and tried to visualize the lean modern skyscraper as a replacement house of worship for the old damaged edifice that still stood with its gaping wounds open to the sky. He wasn't able to do so. He did, however, succeed in assimilating some bit of the atmosphere of Berlin, and that was what he sought most of all. He wandered about for some time, putting pieces together in his mind and trying to dig below the visible surface of the city. It would take weeks to do that, but he still tried, and to a fractional degree he succeeded.

When he returned to the hotel to freshen up before dinner, there was no indication whatever that any incident had taken place. He asked about a ticket to the Philharmonic — he had hoped to hear von Karajan, but there was no concert scheduled. He accepted a recommendation as to a good restaurant and for the lack of anything else to do allowed himself to be booked for a nightclub tour.

A good and thoroughly substantial dinner materially eased his concern. He even enjoyed the group swing through some of the larger Berlin clubs; the schedule had been laid out strictly for tourists, but it was satisfactory nonetheless. When he returned to the Schweitzerhof Nesbitt was even ready to take on a police inquiry if that proved necessary. It did not—nothing whatever was said to him other than a polite good-night when he was handed his attaché case and his key.

His room was just as he had left it, apart from the fact that the chambermaid had turned down his bed, put the night light on, and had left a bit of chocolate neatly wrapped on his pillow. That was enough to convince him that the incident of the afternoon was no longer his concern, but he took the precaution of checking his suitcase to see if the knife was still there.

It was — and he had to restrain an impulse to examine it. He wisely left it strictly alone and went to bed with the thought that enough had already happened for one day.

When he was called in the morning, he was ready to put the city behind him. It took him only twenty minutes to be out in the corridor with his bag, which he took down himself in the elevator. At the desk he paid his bill, expressed his appreciation to Herr Gombert, and took a taxi to the airport. Berlin had been an experience, but the feeling gnawed at him that the whole thing concerning the search of his room had passed off almost too easily. He told himself once more that he had only surprised a sneak thief and that the man, if he had recovered himself in time, had been only too glad to make his escape from the premises. And he could well have done that from the basement.

Once he was airborne and the jet he was riding was boring its way higher and higher above the communist-held territory below, he managed to shake the whole thing off. He turned his thoughts deliberately toward the pater noster, the human vertical conveyor he had seen in the Springer Building.

He took his attaché case onto his lap and prepared to work. His case was a part of him despite the fact that there were tens of thousands of others almost identical to it, literally around the world. To mark his own he had attached a single hotel sticker in one corner, but he had no real need of it. He knew the left-side latch that stuck slightly, the tiny dent in the handle that he had felt a thousand times with his forefinger when he was carrying it. Its very familiarity gave him an added measure of confidence.

He put mundane considerations out of his mind as he unleashed his active imagination and began to shape the possible adventures of Mark Day in Berlin. One episode was already completed, he had lived through it and no further elaboration was necessary. But where he had gladly left that unpleasantness behind him, Mark Day was able to take it in stride. He bent to his work, shaping and planning with a degree of concentration that was close to complete. He was still tightly wrapped in his thoughts when a stewardess touched him on the shoulder and pointed toward the seat-belt sign.

The huge terminal at Frankfurt-am-Main was made up of a series of buildings, all of which were crowded with activity. Trans-Atlantic flights, both civilian and military, maintained a constant flow, interspersed with arrivals and departures for almost every part of the European continent. Although his luggage had been checked through to Vienna, Nesbitt found it necessary to make his way from one busy building to another in order to check in for his Lufthansa flight. When he found the proper counter there was a line ahead of him; he had a fast impression that the whole population of the surrounding area was en route to one place or another. He had never seen so much traffic in his life, not even at Kennedy on a busy Friday night.

When at last he was first in line and could present his ticket, he was greeted with a mild surprise. The airline clerk spoke to him in excellent English, "Mr. Nesbitt, there is a young lady who has been waiting here to see you for some time. Do you wish to speak with her?"

Nesbitt had no idea who it might be: he knew no one in Frankfurt and his travel plans had not been generally disclosed. Curiosity took hold of him for a moment and dictated his decision, "Yes, if there is time."

The clerk nodded. "You have at least forty-five minutes before you board, and there may be a short delay in addition; the aircraft is receiving some maintenance." When he had finished he raised his arm and gestured toward the waiting area. Nesbitt turned and watched, expecting anything from an elderly forgotten aunt to Celestine Van Damm.

The young woman who came forward in response to the clerk's signal was neither, but in her own way she was spectacular. As she approached the counter Nesbitt was acutely aware that beneath the clothing she wore there was a very feminine body indeed; he could not have put it into words, but she was the epitome of sex without appearing to be in the least overt about it. When he reached the point of examining her features he was aware of glowing eyes, moist lips, and a distinct aura of high voltage. She was definitely something. His attention was so riveted on her he failed to notice the camera-equipped young man who followed at an appropriate distance.

The clerk handed him back his ticket together with a boarding pass. "Your flight will be announced in plenty of time, Mr. Nesbitt," he said. He looked carefully one more time at the girl who was approaching and imagined for a moment that he too someday would become a celebrated author.

When the young woman was close enough to do so she greeted Nesbitt in a voice that matched the liquid flow of her body. "Mr. Nesbitt? I am Gretel Hoffmeister; if you can grant me the time, I have been sent to interview you."

At that moment Ed Nesbitt wished that he had at his disposal the urbane suavity of Mark Day, but he could only be himself. "All right," he answered.

The girl turned toward her companion who was waiting patiently behind her. "This is Horst, my photographer."

Nesbitt had been prepared to hear the word "husband" and was minutely relieved that it was not so. He shook hands while receiving a correct Germanic bow and then made a suggestion. "Shall we have some coffee?"

He did not really want any, but he did not like to be interviewed standing in the middle of a crowded terminal.

"We are delighted, Mr. Nesbitt, but my paper will pay for it; we insist."

She turned, and Nesbitt found that she was directly beside him. "You must forgive me," Gretel said, "I am trying to be very professional, but I am a *very big* fan of yours."

25

She managed the flattering emphasis without overdoing it. Automatically Nesbitt followed her into the busy coffee shop and then somehow found a place where the three of them could sit together. The photographer was agreeable enough, but he did not intrude into the conversation. As soon as the order had been placed he got to his feet and slightly to Nesbitt's embarrassment unslung his Leica and began to take a series of candid shots.

Nesbitt could do very little about it; he knew that he looked abominable in candid photographs and that they seemed always to emphasize his worst features. He endured the discomfort for a minute or two and then, to his relief, Horst sat down once more, apparently satisfied.

While he answered the usual questions concerning himself and his books for the next twenty minutes, Nesbitt also took stock of the young woman who was taking down her notes on reporter's foolscap, concentrating on her work. She was close enough to him to make him aware of the heat of her body, an invitation at the same time both offered and denied. At least at that time and place. She was neither pretty nor beautiful, but she was astonishingly attractive. Her voice was a major asset and once more he wished that he had at least a small measure of the European skill at languages. She had an accent, of course, but she was never at a loss for words in English and it was very seldom that she chose the wrong one.

It never occurred to him to wonder how old she was; it did not matter. When he was granted a respite while she caught up on her notes, he saw himself as one member of a bridge foursome playing on the terrace of a villa somewhere on the warm and sunny Mediterranean coast. The other three would be Mark Day, Celestine, and this young woman — minus the photographer, of course. He was a better than average bridge player and he had been complimented many times on his game.

Presently Gretel was finished; for a moment she hesitated, and Nesbitt anticipated the usual request for an autographed book.

"Mr. Nesbitt," she said. "May I ask one more favor of you? It is really for Lufthansa; they have asked if you will be kind enough to take a picture with their aircraft. They have one ready, and a stewardess to be with you."

"If they would like," Nesbitt replied. He knew that such publicity was always a help, and would also be appreciated by Ullstein Verlag. He was before the public and his reputation was a large part of his stock-in-trade.

"It is not necessary that you bring your case," Gretel suggested as he reached for it. "You can leave it with Horst; it will be completely safe."

"Isn't he going to take the picture?"

"No, Lufthansa has their own man."

Nesbitt glanced at his watch; he still had ten minutes before the plane was scheduled to start loading and there was a possible delay on top of that. He did not believe that the German airline would fly off without him while he was posing for a publicity picture at the company's request. Satisfied, he handed over his case and followed his guide through a series of gateways until they were on the field level. There he was escorted toward a waiting aircraft where a photographer armed with a Rolleiflex was standing at the foot of the stairs.

Nesbitt would have welcomed the chance at least to comb his hair, but it was not to be. "The stewardess, she comes," the photographer said and nodded back toward

27

the gate. The girl who was hurrying out was, even at a distance, an obvious model; the very way she carried herself told Nesbitt that, and the way that she protected her hair against the slight breeze. At the top of the steps two stewardesses who were already on the aircraft looked out. They were both attractive girls, but clearly this was a case where a professional was being called in.

That opinion was confirmed when she arrived and at once struck an absolutely correct pose, decorating the shot but leaving Nesbitt clearly as the central figure.

The session took five minutes, the photographer cranking a total of eight exposures into his camera. "It is good," he announced when he was finished. "From these a good one we will have."

Nesbitt turned to find that Gretel had rejoined him. "They have just called your flight," she announced. "You can go directly to your plane from here, it is arranged. Horst will meet us with your case."

It was all entirely correct, but for a moment a brief hint of suspicion came to Nesbitt; he took a quick mental inventory of the contents of his case and remembered that almost all of his traveler's checks were in it — and they added up to a considerable amount. Before he could develop that thought further he saw the photographer coming through a gateway, the case in his hand. At the foot of the stairs of the Vienna-bound aircraft it was delivered to him with another slight Germanic bow.

Gretel handed him a card. "Please be kind enough to remember me," she said. "It is to me a great event to meet you."

Nesbitt smiled. "I have enjoyed it also," he answered, and then impulsively he added, "very much."

The girl held out her hand, "Auf Wiedersehen," she offered, "You are really very like Mark Day himself."

The rest of the passengers were coming, a single file passing through the gate and advancing toward the Boeing 737. Nesbitt looked once again at the remarkably desirable girl who was his confessed fan. Then he thanked Horst for his help, took the offered hand from Gretel and contented himself with giving it a gentle squeeze. As he turned to climb the steps into the aircraft, he allowed himself to hope that at some time, in some way, he would see her again.

Departure was entirely normal and on time to the minute. Because the load was reasonably light Nesbitt had no one seated next to him, which allowed him a place to leave his attaché case.

The thought of his previous concern came to him; since he was now totally safe from observation from the ground, he carefully put his case on his lap and opened it. As he did so he automatically flicked his left hand against the brace that held the lid open; on that side it had developed a slight weakness. This time, however, it behaved properly.

He checked the contents and found them intact. His traveler's checks, with his neat notation on the current folder showing how many of the checks he had used, were undisturbed. A look through the pockets in the lid revealed everything to be exactly as he had left it, even to the antacid pills that he kept on the right-hand side of the first compartment.

Relieved, he closed his case once more and thumped the locking lever that always stuck.

This time it did not.

It invariably had — at least for months. He tried it again

to make sure, but the customary slight malfunction did not appear.

He took the case in his right hand as he always carried it, the hotel sticker toward the outside, and felt for the slight irregularity on the handle he knew so well. It was not there.

One thing could have been accidental: two would have been very remote. Three was impossible. It was not his own attaché case.

3

HERR SCHOLZ of the Hotel Intercontinental Vienna was all
attention and courtesy. He invited Nesbitt to sit down and
saw that he was served with a cup of excellent coffee almost at once. His English was effortless, in addition to
which he was obviously exactly the kind of man Nesbitt
had hoped he would be.

"We are delighted to have you with us," Herr Scholz declared. "You are as famous here, of course, as you are
everywhere else. I have enjoyed many of your fine books
myself. As a matter of fact, I was on the point of writing
you a letter."

That was interesting. "What about?" Nesbitt asked.

"In our restaurant we have a new little idea: we are

creating a series of gourmet sandwiches to be named after celebrated detectives of literature. The most important will be the Sherlock Holmes, after that the Lord Peter Wimsey, the Miss Marple, a very huge one which will be the Nero Wolfe, the Virgil Tibbs, which is to be dark meat of turkey, and, hopefully, the Mark Day. Obviously we must have your permission first."

Nesbitt was genuinely pleased. "Granted," he said. "Mark Day isn't a detective in the classic sense, but if you feel that he fits, go ahead."

"Thank you. It will be served with a cup of Dutch chocolate in honor of Miss Van Damm. Now, allow me to ask if you will dine with Mrs. Scholz and myself this evening; we would be most pleased if you can accept."

Nesbitt did, then he turned to the business at hand. "Herr Scholz, as you know I write fiction about international espionage, but I don't apply the same sort of imagination to my private life."

"I would not expect so."

"I'm glad, because I have something to tell you and I want very much to be believed. Yesterday, in Berlin, I returned unexpectedly to my room to find my luggage being searched."

"The police took such a liberty?"

"It wasn't the police, Herr Scholz — quite the contrary. I dismissed it as probably a petty thief."

"The management, then...."

"I dealt with the matter myself, which I must ask you to regard as confidential."

"Absolutely."

"Secondly, while I was changing planes today in Frankfurt my attaché case was switched for another. Not by mistake — the contents were carefully transferred apparently in the hope I would not notice."

"Have you considered the possibility of an elaborate practical joke?"

"I have; it won't fit. Something is happening to me, Herr Scholz, that I don't understand."

Scholz wrote rapidly on a pad before him. "I will alert our security people immediately; they are very efficient. Also I would like your permission to move you to a special suite we have for distinguished visitors; it has some special protective devices. The rate will be the same, of course."

"I wasn't asking for that."

"I know, Mr. Nesbitt, this is at our request. May I ask what your plans are now?"

"I'd like to visit the American Embassy."

"Good. It is on Boltzmanngasse; I will have a car take you there."

Normally Ed Nesbitt had little difficulty getting along with almost anyone, but the young man who received him at the embassy was something of a special case. Apparently somewhere in his early thirties, he was tall, slender, and distinguished by a moustache that seemed to have ambitions of becoming a true handlebar. As he leaned back in his office chair he was entirely courteous, but at the same time he maintained a certain cool reserve that Nesbitt found distracting.

"It is an interesting account, Mr. Nesbitt," he said, "but you can understand that I find it a bit fanciful."

"So do I," Nesbitt agreed, "but I assure you that it's accurate."

The embassy man picked up a pencil and toyed with it. There was nothing wrong in that, but it still gave Nesbitt the feeling that the man before him wasn't giving him his full attention. When he spoke, there was a suggestion of weariness in his voice. "What is it precisely that you want us to do?"

Nesbitt was determined not to make the same mistake himself; he tried his best to sound reasonable and business-like. "I'm not asking you to do anything, Mr. Windress. I'm trying to provide some information you might wish to have."

If Windress was in any way impressed, he concealed it completely. "Your name is well known," he said, "and so are the stories that you write. I'm sure that they're very entertaining, despite the fact that from time to time they have caused us some concern."

"In what way?" Nesbitt asked.

Windress preferred to ignore the question. "I accept the fact that you surprised a thief in your hotel room in Berlin, but fortunately you were not injured and apparently nothing was taken. As for your case, the type you have there is extremely common; you just told me that you have the sticker of a rather remote hotel on it for purposes of identification. I find it difficult to understand how another one could be found to substitute for it on short notice."

The words were reasonable and Nesbitt knew it, but something in the tone of their delivery annoyed him. He gave it a second's thought and decided that he was being patronized, something that always set his teeth on edge. It usually came from people who pretended to be very superior about his work, but who probably read Fu Manchu in secret. "Are you interested in a knife with fingerprints on it?" he asked.

"I believe that is a matter for the police."

"I see." Nesbitt tried one more time. "Is it your position, then, that what I have told you is of no special interest to you or to the embassy?"

Windress dropped the mask since his visitor had stated the matter so clearly. "More or less, yes."

"Then will you be kind enough to answer one more question?"

Windress tossed down the pencil. "If I can, yes."

Nesbitt stood up, his case in his hand. "How do I get to see someone with some brains around here?"

The Deputy Chief of the Mission answered the description; Nesbitt knew that the moment that he met him and shook hands. The senior diplomat was relaxed in the manner of a man who has no need to put up a front of any kind. He was in his shirt-sleeves as he settled down and waved his guest to a chair. "I hear that you have a problem," he said, and leaned back to listen.

Very shortly it was clear that his attention was complete. When Nesbitt had finished he sat up straight once more. "By any chance do you have the knife with you?" he asked.

Nesbitt produced it, still carefully wrapped in the clean handkerchief. "I'm sorry, sir, I didn't catch your name."

"Morgan."

"Thank you. Mr. Morgan, please believe that this isn't the kind of plaything I carry around for amusement. Customs might question it."

"I'm surprised you got it into Austria. May I keep it for a little while?"

"Of couse. I have another exhibit: the card that Miss Gretel Hoffmeister gave me this morning. If you want a bet, I'll give you three to one that it doesn't check out."

"Why?"

"First, because her confederate switched my case. Secondly, notice the card itself." Nesbitt took it out of his wallet and passed it over. "It gives her name and the title 'feature reporter.' That isn't standard newspaper nomenclature — I've seen too many cards. Also there isn't any masthead logo."

Morgan touched a button and his secretary came in. "Hanna," he said, "phone through to Frankfurt and check on the identity of this person. Let me know as soon as you have an answer."

When she had gone Morgan put another question. "Why do you think they would want to switch cases with you?"

Nesbitt was ready for that one. "I can offer one suggestion: nothing was taken, but perhaps something was added."

Morgan took a moment to consider the idea. "How sure are you that a switch was actually made?" he asked.

"I'm positive. Before I came here I reexamined the case minutely — it isn't mine. I've had my own more than five years and have carried it constantly. I checked very carefully on six more identifying marks which are on my own case, and all six were missing. The cover of my own case tore once slightly and I glued it back. The repair should be right here." He tapped the spot.

"Who else have you told this to?"

"Herr Scholz at the Intercontinental and Windress — that's all."

"I know Peter Scholz; he's completely reliable. Windress at least knows enough to keep his mouth shut."

"Do you want to have this case examined?"

Morgan shook his head. "Let's find out first about your lady friend in Frankfurt. Coffee?"

"No, thanks. Shall I wait outside?"

"It's more comfortable here. The *Herald Trib* is there if you haven't seen it."

Nesbitt settled down with the newspaper to catch up with what was going on throughout the world. When he had done that, he checked the stock tables and looked up the values of several securities. Next he turned to the book section and was well into the reviews when Morgan's secretary came back in.

"There isn't any such reporter in Frankfurt," she said. "Also, I learned that none of the papers sent anyone to interview Mr. Nesbitt; they didn't know he was coming through. That is also true of the principal magazines. They are very sure there is no Gretel Hoffmeister in the business in Frankfurt; if there were, they would know of her."

"Thank you," Morgan said, and watched while she closed the door behind her. Then he spoke to Nesbitt. "What's your first name?"

"Edwin."

"All right, Ed, I'm convinced that someone went to the trouble of looking up your schedule and had a phony card printed up. It could be a prank, but it isn't likely. I'll check on that Lufthansa picture; it may tell us something more. Now you said that something might have been *added* to your briefcase."

"Yes. It occurred to me that since I'm on a round-the-world trip, and that has been publicized, someone might have chosen me to be an unknowing courier. In other words — a dummy."

"Put something in your case for you to deliver without knowing it to some other part of the world?"

"Yes."

Morgan shook his head. "It would have to be something very light, so that you wouldn't notice the change in weight, and thin enough to fit into the lining somewhere. That could be easily mailed."

"True," Nesbitt agreed, "but whenever you mail something, you have to put an address on it. I realize how much stuff is in the mail constantly all over the world, but that doesn't mean that certain addresses can't be watched. I'm sure that some of them are."

For a long moment it was quiet while Morgan made up his mind. "I want to check up on some more things," he said finally. "I'd like to have that card the woman gave you in Frankfurt."

"Of course."

Morgan wrote on a slip of paper. "If anything more happens to you, I want to know immediately. I'm giving you my private home number. Also, please call me here tomorrow sometime after ten. If I ask you to come in, bring your case with you."

Nesbitt thanked him and left. He went back to his hotel with the feeling that behind his back some wires were already humming; Morgan was not the type of man to discount him simply because he made his living writing popular literature.

In his absence his room had been changed to a very de

luxe suite; the first thing that he noticed was the special lock on the door. When he was inside and had visited the bathroom, he sat down with a nail file from his toilet kit and the substitute case that held his papers. With some care he filed off the inside corner of one of the small studs on the bottom. After that he opened the case and marked the aluminum edging in three different places. Finally he filed a small nick in the handle where he could conveniently feel it at any time. With that job out of the way he stretched out on the bed and took some rest before it was time to go down to dinner.

When he reached the dining room, he found three people waiting for him. Herr Scholz and his wife were there, and with them a very presentable young lady. As the introductions were performed, Nesbitt learned that his unexpected dinner companion was Miss Frieda Müller who was on Herr Scholz's staff. Her English was quite heavily accented, but she used the language easily and her manner was delightful.

"I am very happy to meet such a famous man," she said when they were seated. "What brings you to Vienna, Herr Nesbitt?"

"First of all the great charm and reputation of the city," Ed answered her. "Also I'm doing some research on backgrounds for future books."

"So we may expect that any time now Mark Day will be checking into our hotel!"

"Very possibly."

"If he happens to bring Miss Van Damm with him," Herr Scholz said, "we shall try to be very broad-minded about the situation. Vienna is, after all, a city of much gayety."

The dinner was an excellent one and the conversation was spirited. Nesbitt learned that Frieda Müller spoke four languages easily. "It is my work to be a special guide for our most distinguished guests," she explained. "Many times they wish to go places that are unusual and, of course, they seldom take part in group tours since their schedules do not permit."

"Someday I would like to be important enough to rate that kind of attention," Nesbitt remarked.

"Oh, but you do! That is why tonight I have the great pleasure of your company."

"It is our misfortune to be engaged after dinner," Scholz said, "but Miss Müller is not. If you would like, it has been arranged that she will take you out for a little night tour of our fascinating city."

Nothing could have suited Nesbitt better than that and he said so. Despite the fact that he was past his supposedly most romantic years, he had not lost an iota of his appreciation of attractive feminine company, and Frieda Müller was particularly charming. During the time that the ladies excused themselves after dinner he went quickly to the cashier's window and changed two traveler's checks into Austrian currency. Since he was being regarded as a celebrity, it was up to him to fill the role properly.

In a quite elegant car provided by the hotel they went first to the amusement park to see and ride the giant Ferris wheel. It was a fascinating piece of equipment and Nesbitt ached to do something with it; unfortunately it was off limits since it had already been used in the unforgettable film, *The Third Man*.

The wine gardens of Grinzing took on a special glow thanks to the presence of Frieda, who had the wonderful ability to fit herself into his evening, sensing his every change of mood and responding to each one. He allowed himself to wonder if the "Miss" was purely a professional designation; she was far too attractive a girl to have been overlooked and she did not in any way impress him as frigid.

Because he wanted to know, he asked. "I am divorced," she told him. "Because I was abandoned, the court allowed me back my maiden name. So now I am single."

"I regret to tell you this," Nesbitt said, "but I fear that your former husband has met with misfortune."

Frieda turned to him and seized his arm. "*What is it that you know?*" she demanded.

He was ashamed of himself; that was not the reaction he had expected. Because he had no other choice, he finished as he had planned. "I know only that no free man in his right mind would ever abandon you."

Gradually her fingers loosened their grip and the fright ebbed out of her; then they tightened once more. "You are very kind," she said. He was spared having to respond to that by the small strolling orchestra that stopped at their table. The violinist drew his bow across the strings and summoned up the magic of Johann Strauss, Jr. The accordionist sang and Nesbitt felt the warmth of Frieda's body next to his own. The wine helped, and it was served by the tumblerful to speed the process of consumption. He knew that it had loosened his inhibitions — he would never have said a thing like that while he was fully sober — but he did not regret what he had done. Frieda seemed closer than she had been, although he had not seen her move, and he had very definite thoughts about her.

"We can go now if you like to the basement of the city

hall," she proposed. "There are several places there and in one of them there is very good music, beer, and *Gemütlichkeit*. Do you know that word?"

"Yes, I do," he answered, "Let's go."

The restaurant was low-ceilinged, long, and somewhat noisy, but it was the kind of noise that spoke of good times being had and Nesbitt was happy. Shortly after he and his companion were seated the small orchestra broke into energetic melody and some of the patrons began to sing, venting their spirits whether they were in tune or not. Nesbitt ordered beer and relishes; the evening would have been nothing without Frieda there to share it with him and banish all thoughts of his recent experiences from his mind. He understood that she was a professional hostess for the hotel, but it seemed to him that their relationship was a bit warmer than the bare responsibilities of duty. As she chatted with him he forgot her accent and measured her in his mind as a possible heroine for a forthcoming book. She would do nicely, he decided, and that added still another plus to the evening.

The thought entered his mind that perhaps she was expected to be more cordial still, but the image of Herr Scholz shattered that thought — such a man would never have arranged the evening for him with a woman of that type. If Frieda Müller ever went to bed with him it would be because she wanted it too, and it would be an arrangement between friends. Much as she attracted him, he knew that for many reasons he would not make the first move.

When they at last left the Bierstube he offered to show her home. "It is not necessary," she assured him. "I have a room at the hotel that is for me always ready." She looked at him. "You will forgive me if I do not invite you to share it?"

Nesbitt smiled at her and took her hand. "You have given me so much already," he said.

She looked bedroom eyes at him. "How long will you be in Vienna?" she asked.

"Not very long, I'm afraid."

"Then, please, you will come back?"

He felt the pressure of her fingers. "I want to," he answered.

He left her in the lobby after saying the proper things and went up to his suite, to think and perhaps to dream. He came back to reality long enough to check the attaché case — apparently it had not been touched. That was enough: he undressed and went to bed with the unashamed thought that one day the empty pillow on the other side would have Frieda's head on it, and for that realization he would not trade places with Mark Day or anyone else.

In the morning he phoned Morgan as directed and was asked to come in as soon as convenient. He left immediately and was back in the senior diplomat's office a short time later.

Morgan came directly to the point. "One thing you didn't tell me yesterday: how in the hell did you get the drop on that man you found in your room in Berlin? There's quite a file on him — and he's considered very dangerous."

"I guess I was lucky," Nesbitt said.

Morgan studied him. "It had to be more than that. I'm going to ask you a question in absolute confidence and I want a candid answer: precisely what is your status?"

"Private citizen, that's it. I'm not concealing anything."

"Yet you took an armed man who is a well-known professional with your bare hands? Come on, Nesbitt, I know that you're who you say you are, but there's got to be more to it than that."

"There isn't."

"Very well, if you say so. The Agency people can fill me in. Meanwhile, we'd like a look at that attaché case."

Nesbitt emptied it out and handed it over. Morgan rang for his secretary and gave it to her without any instructions. The girl accepted it and left.

From a container on a table behind him Morgan poured out two cups of coffee. "I'm sorry to interfere with your plans," he said, "but I'll have to ask you to stay here for a little while."

"No problem."

"Good. You can understand it's a little hard for some people to swallow the idea that a popular writer of spy thrillers is himself innocently caught up in an espionage situation. And you're sufficiently prominent; I don't think you were mistaken for someone else."

"I thought of that possibility," Nesbitt said.

"I'm sure that you did. Meantime they're holding a man in Berlin who probably has a helluva bellyache."

"Am I in trouble back there?" Nesbitt asked.

"Not with the police, if that's what you mean. Actually you have them a little awed."

There was a rap on the door. Morgan opened it to admit a man in a well-cut business suit who looked the typical successful American — that was as much as Nesbitt could gather as he waited to be introduced.

"George, this is Mr. Nesbitt." Morgan was casual.

The man shook hands. "My name is Smith," he said. "It really is."

After Nesbitt had settled down again, Morgan continued. "Mr. Smith is very interested in some of the information you gave me yesterday. He is with the government; you can trust him completely."

For ten minutes the men talked, but it was mainly a retracing of the ground Nesbitt had already covered. Smith asked a number of questions, but if he had any doubts about what Nesbitt was telling him, he gave no indication whatever.

When the intercom buzzed, Morgan picked up his phone. "Yes," he said, and then listened. For fifteen or twenty seconds it was quiet in the office, then he spoke a word of thanks and hung up.

He looked at Nesbitt. "You're entitled to know this: we found your case most interesting, and I'm convinced that you didn't plant anything in it yourself. Pardon my directness, but it's the best way. George?"

Smith took over. "Mr. Nesbitt, I'll come right to the point too; are you willing to cooperate with us?"

Mark Day would have been a little careful about that, and Nesbitt was too. "Who's us?" he asked.

"The United States Government."

Smith said it casually without any dramatics, which gave Nesbitt only one choice. "All right — of course," he said.

"Good. Let's start with a copy of your itinerary."

"I have one here." Nesbitt located it easily among his papers and handed it over.

"Thank you," Smith acknowledged. "It may just be that you have put us onto something in which we are very much interested. I would like you to continue exactly as before — doing just what you have already planned. Please try to put out of your mind the idea that the case you're carrying isn't actually your own — adopt it. Don't under any circumstances betray the fact that you know a switch has been made."

"Herr Scholz knows."

"I'm aware of that; we've already spoken to Peter about it and he will say nothing. He is passing off the security on your suite as routine for a famous visitor."

"How about his own people?"

"They understand that some of your books have annoyed the Iron Curtain people, hence the precautions against a possible incident in the hotel."

"That sounds valid," Nesbitt said. "And there's some truth in it."

"Now, Mr. Nesbitt, something more. We're going to leave your case exactly as it is. Somewhere along your route it may be switched back or simply stolen; in that case we will want to know immediately."

"How will I contact you?"

"You won't have any problem. We're going to keep tabs on you for a little while — I hope you don't mind."

"You mean, I'll be under surveillance?"

"Yes, but don't let it cramp your style; I guarantee you against any embarrassment."

Nesbitt had his doubts about that, but he didn't voice them. "When will it all start?" he asked.

"Very soon, just don't worry about it."

There was another tap on the door; then Morgan's secretary came in carrying Nesbitt's empty attaché case. He took it and installed his papers back in their proper places.

46

"I'd like to have some way of signaling whoever is going to be covering me if I have to," he said.

"I'll be in touch with you again shortly," Smith told him. "Whatever is behind all this, we want to know. And so do you."

"Of course, but I doubt if you'll tell me."

Smith smiled. "We'll do the best that we feel we can if the occasion arises. Just don't put it into a book afterwards."

"I won't," Nesbitt promised.

That ended it for all practical purposes. Nesbitt downed the last of his coffee, said the proper things, and left. As he rode back to the hotel, the attaché case on his lap, he knew that it contained something — his guess had been right on that — but what? He had no idea whatever. He thought of the wild idea that it might have been transformed into some kind of a booby trap, using the same type of explosive that certain terrorists had used for their letter bombs, but that was too far out to be realistic, despite the fact that he was scheduled to meet with some prominent political personalities.

He picked up his mail at the hotel desk and then went directly up to his suite. He had only been there a minute or two when the phone rang. That meant that whoever the caller was, he had first been filtered through Herr Scholz's office — it was part of the security routine. He picked up the instrument and said, "Yes?"

Herr Scholz himself was on the line. "Mr. Nesbitt, there is a lady here waiting to see you in the lobby. I gather that she has a luncheon appointment with you although she didn't say so directly."

A mental image of the girl who had called herself Gretel

Hoffmeister came into Nesbitt's mind, and he was cautious. "What name did she give?" he asked.

Herr Scholz seemed to be amused, or perhaps surprised. "It is quite remarkable, Mr. Nesbitt, but she says that she is Miss Celestine Van Damm."

4

MORE THAN ANY OTHER living person Ed Nesbitt knew that there was no Celestine Van Damm; he had created her out of his own imagination for the sole purpose of providing Mark Day with a suitable girl friend. He had chosen her name for its European sound and the good probability that out of the earth's entire population there would be no one so called. Van Damm was common enough in Dutch circles, but Celestine was as unlikely as anything he had been able to think of when he had first sketched her out on paper. In the course of several books she had indeed become almost real to him; he had told the people in Berlin that he would know her if he met her. That was true. But she was fictional nonetheless.

Therefore his good sense told him that whoever was in the lobby had simply used that name to pique his curiosity. He admitted to himself that it was a good device, good enough that he was going to go and have a look. It would be interesting to see what someone else thought that that mythical young woman looked like. He informed Herr Scholz that he would be right down, ran a comb through his hair, and headed for the lobby.

He saw her almost as soon as he was out of the elevator and the effect was startling. She was sitting in one of the comfortable chairs her legs crossed, her arms resting easily on the upholstery. He had said that he would know her if he saw her, and, dammit, he did. She was the epitome of what he had conceived and there she was before him, as real as the intoxicating city that surrounded them both. Even if she was really Mary Glutz from Dubuque, there was no mistaking the dark cascading hair, the exotic almond eyes, the high cheekbones, and the aristocratic air that clung to her like the pulse of life itself. It had no arrogance in it; it was fine breeding as though she had been in some previous incarnation a high-spirited race-horse born to challenge the wind itself. If the girl he saw was not the one who had sent for him, then the whole world of illusion in which he earned his living had betrayed him.

He stepped to the desk and spoke to the concierge. "I believe that a lady is asking for me," he said.

"Mr. Nesbitt? Allow me, sir, my congratulations. I have somehow imagined that Miss Van Damm did not really exist. Forgive me."

He looked over Nesbitt's shoulder, feasting his eyes quite openly. Nesbitt turned and saw that the girl he had known would be the right one was at that moment approaching him. In two or three seconds she was close enough to hold out her hand. "So nice to see you again," she said. Her voice had the haunting huskiness that he had described dozens of times in print, striving always to find the right words to describe it — the reediness that had shot one or two gifted British actresses to stardom.

His next words did not consciously come from his brain — it was as though he was playing a role himself. "I believe we have a luncheon engagement."

She gave him a pulse-pounding smile. "I have been looking forward to it," she responded, again in that distinctive voice.

At that moment a famous incident leaped into Nesbitt's mind: the scene many years before when Sir Arthur Conan Doyle had stood waiting on a station platform to greet a guest he had never met. As William Gillette had stepped off the train, at that historic moment Sir Arthur had, for the first time, seen the living embodiment of Sherlock Holmes.

As they walked toward the dining room the demon of distraction asked in Nesbitt's ear if he was being taken for a sucker once again. He answered silently and decisively that if he was, it was worth the price.

In the dining room they were seated with proper ceremony. Without asking Nesbitt ordered the drinks; he specified Miss Van Damm's established favorite as he had chosen it for her and amused himself by taking Mark Day's most likely choice for himself. Then he watched as his astonishing companion removed her gloves and made herself comfortable. "I wonder," she began, "if you remember the first time that we met."

Nesbitt mentioned the book in which Mark Day had first encountered the Dutch heiress, but she shook her head. "It was well before that," she said.

"Then you must have been a little girl."

She smiled again and shamed the Mona Lisa. "How nice. But it was actually at a party — on Long Island. Does that help you?"

A dim and long-buried memory began to take uncertain shape.

"I was rather young at the time, and you had just published your first book. That made you the lion and I captured you for a little while."

The focus became less blurred and the first light of realization began to dawn.

"I brought you a drink," he said.

"Yes, and you wondered, out loud I might add, if I was old enough to have it."

"That was bad manners, but accurate observation," Nesbitt told her. "You weren't."

"Anyhow, I must have made an impression, because when I picked up your new book some little time after that, there I was."

There was a temporary hiatus, an interval which allowed Nesbitt to wonder if he had unintentionally committed libel — for Celestine Van Damm had frequently been to bed with Mark Day and he had said so in print.

"Let's go back to the beginning," he proposed. "What is your real name — honest and truly?"

"Van Damm. I can prove it if you want me to."

He took a minute while he thought about that. He had believed that Celestine Van Damm had been created out of thin air, now he knew better. He had actually met her, then had forgotten. But she had made an impression, one that had lingered in his unconscious mind until he had called it back under the mistaken idea that he was being freshly creative.

"Do you mind?" he asked.

She quirked her lips. "No, although I have to keep telling people that I'm not an archeologist."

Nesbitt meshed his fingers. "Three or four years ago, for a story sequence, I dreamed up a Spanish beauty — a classic one with a family that went back for generations. I called her Flavia Alvarez de Toledo."

"That's beautiful."

"Yes, but I couldn't use it — I remembered just in time that it's the title of one of Virgil Thomson's musical portraits."

The arrival of the drinks halted things for a few moments and gave him time to think. When they were alone once more he was ready to continue. "Look, your real first name isn't Celestine, I'm pretty sure of that."

"You're right, but it's not too different."

"Never mind that: you announced yourself as Miss Celestine Van Damm. So may I call you Celestine?"

"Of course."

"How about the 'miss'?"

She nodded. "That's true. So is something else — the family money. Not stupendous, but enough to keep the fortune hunters circling overhead. It's made me a little wary."

He left it at that. She could have been previously married, but it didn't matter; he was so far ahead of the game he could afford to pass a few bets. "I'm sorry about one thing," he said. "I can't produce Mark Day for you. I never admit it to myself, but I'll tell you — he doesn't exist."

She looked at him over the top of her glass. "You'll do."

That snapped back on him like a taut rubber band. "Don't, please. Just recently in Berlin I explained in detail that I'm not Mark Day. I pointed out the differences. Look at me: I'm over forty, only average height, ten pounds too heavy, and I'm certainly not a secret agent."

"I think you could keep secrets very well," she told him. "I would trust you."

That made it harder. "Thank you, but it just won't fit. I know too much about Mark Day."

She moved her shoulders in a way that dismissed the words he had just spoken. "That isn't the point," she said. "You see, I like you."

When the lunch was over and he knew that he would have to go about his business, he tried almost desperately to think what he should say to her in parting. They might never meet again, but her face would haunt him every time that he rolled a fresh sheet of paper into his typewriter. She solved it for him by opening the topic herself. "Where are you going from here?" she asked.

"Prague, I have a publisher there."

"Will they let you take your earnings out of the country?"

"No, I have to spend them."

"Then you know about the wonderful crystal that they have. And the fine suedes."

"I plan to have a look. How about you?"

"Well," she answered, "at the moment I'm not quite sure.

54

But would it bother you too much if I made it a point to look you up now and then?"

Ed Nesbitt had long dreamed of seeing Prague; to him the city typified central Europe and the fairy-tale atmosphere that still clung stubbornly to its old-world architecture and cobbled squares. At the same time he knew that there was an under city — one that often boiled with intrigue and the discipline inflicted in the Iron Curtain countries. He hoped that he would be able to sense some of this and resolved to miss nothing that came within his range.

The airport did not impress him, but he knew enough not to judge an ancient city by such a modern overlay. The terminal had a certain bleakness he could not define, but he had little time to notice it as he checked through the usual formalities and complied with the regulation that forced him to change some of his dollars into crowns. It was not a large amount, but he knew that a considerable supply of local currency was waiting for him at his publisher's and that none of it could be taken with him. It was part of the cost of his trip and he accepted it at that; perhaps he would be able to buy something that he could dispose of afterwards.

He was turning away from the banking counter when he was confronted by a young man who obviously wanted to speak to him. Nesbitt made a swift appraisal: age in the vicinity of twenty-five, face boyish, figure unusually slender, clothing neat and carefully worn, but poorly cut of inferior material. The tie was a narrow black strip doing its best to appear dignified without the means to do so. Nesbitt had never seen the young man before, but he knew him just the same — one of the limitless army of hopefuls who put on a brave front, learned languages, and hoped to find some way from where they were to the Promised Land. Usually that meant America, sometimes just promotion, but always a burning aspiration for a better life and a more significant one. He had helped several of them on their way and counted the money well spent.

This one fitted the pattern like a key piece in an intricate jigsaw puzzle. He came forward beaming a welcome, but avoiding any hint of familiarity. That might come later. "Mr. Nesbitt?" he asked in a quite good accent, "I have been sent to meet you by your publishers. My name is Josef."

Nesbitt shook hands while he added a few bits of deduction. Josef was probably the translator, or one of them, who had learned his language skill at the university. He had probably starved himself to make it possible. Now he at least had a job, though without question an underpaid one, a glance at his shoes confirmed that. However, there was the possibility that nothing better could be had except at a black market price — and there was not much illicit activity in shoes.

"Allow me, sir, to get your baggage; I will handle it all for you." The young man was bursting with energy, or at least pretending to be; if left alone he would undoubtedly strain himself trying to carry everything without appearing to be inconvenienced in the least. But nevertheless, Nesbitt liked him; he was trying.

He continued to like him even when the young man attempted to relieve him of his attaché case — it could have been an innocent gesture.

A porter was found to handle the luggage and put it into a vehicle which served as a cab. After Nesbitt was inside, his case still firmly in his hands, Josef halted at the curb, his hand still on the door. "May I accompany you, sir?" he asked.

"Of course, come along." Nesbitt moved over a bit more to underline his invitation. Josef got in.

Because it was late in the evening, there was not a great deal to be seen on the way to the hotel. Nesbitt caught the outlines of some massive churches and presumed that they were no longer in use for their original purpose, but he was not certain. He saw that there were street-car tracks and a certain aura of quaintness, but not too much else was clear before they pulled up before the hotel that his travel agent had recommended.

The lobby was about what he had expected — dated, but acceptable, with adequate evidence of cleanliness. He checked in and then gave his attention to his new acquaintance. "Would you like some coffee?" he invited.

Josef hesitated and then took the path of prudence. "Thank you, sir, I believe you may be tired and wish to rest. I shall call upon you in the morning."

"That will be fine," Nesbitt said.

After another brisk handshake in what he hoped was the western manner Josef left, allowing Nesbitt to go up to his room. It was nothing elaborate, but it would do. He unpacked a few things, washed in what he presumed was a de luxe bathroom for Prague and then, just to be sure, checked the identifying marks he had made on the substitute attaché case. It was still the same one.

He glanced at his watch and noted that despite what Josef had said, it was still early. Since his stay in this city would be relatively brief, the idea of a walk occurred to him. There were things to be seen and he wanted to see them. For a moment he wondered if any danger would be involved, then decided that the best way to settle that would be to ask, discreetly, at the desk.

That left the question of the attaché case. He could leave it with the hotel for safekeeping and he would not be burdened with it. The other alternative would be to take it with him and thereby deliberately invite attention. He asked himself what Mark Day would do and got a conclusive answer — Day would have too much sense to go out at night carrying a case he obviously had no need to have with him.

He ran a comb through his hair and rode a venerable elevator down to the lobby, his case in his hand. At the desk he made his manner plain and without ostentation as he handed over his case. "I'm thinking of going out to look around a bit," he said. "I presume that would be all right."

The clerk, who was an elderly man with frizzled hair, understood. His English was painful, but he managed. "Good, why is not. Your bag, you wish to leave?"

Nesbitt handed it over and received an elaborate receipt. It meant nothing, of course, but he accepted it and put it carefully into his wallet. Then he went out the door and stood on the streets of Prague.

Less than five minutes walk took him to the center of the city, a long, rising open rectangle surrounded by buildings that had all probably been in place for many decades past. There were a few places open, restaurants and the like, but otherwise the whole area seemed to be keeping its own peace.

One of Ed Nesbitt's assets was a strong sense of direction; he was very seldom turned around and usually could find his way anywhere. For five or ten minutes he strolled up the wide sidewalk, feeling the others who were there rather than seeing them, and then decided to explore a side street. He had no fear of getting lost or not being able to find his hotel in a country where he knew not one word of the language. He was soaking up impressions of the city and that was what he most wanted.

Before putting his little plan into action he stopped and studied the display in a camera store window. Although a real effort had been made to make the merchandise look attractive, he did not recognize any of the product names. The cameras themselves were all the same — small 35mm. affairs with very little sophistication and a look of cheapness about them despite the careful way they had been put on view. None of the other products appeared to be very good — something which was probably the result of currency restrictions and the requirement to carry only Soviet-bloc offerings. It was a depressing note which he stored carefully away in his memory. Then he turned, and choosing a side street at will, set off to see what he could discover.

He wandered for more than an hour, up one street and down the next, without finding anything that attracted him. It was all routine, or appeared to be, but he had no way of knowing what lay behind the many closed doors that were uniform in telling him nothing. If he could somehow magically know everything there was to know about each of the buildings he passed, he would have enough material for fifty books — but his gleanings were nil. A little of the atmosphere of the city, perhaps, but beyond that nothing more.

It was then that he sensed, or somehow detected, that he was being followed.

The realization did not come to him all at once, it built up by slow increments in his subconscious without his being aware of it at all. Then, as certain minute things forced themselves into his mind, the suspicion grew rapidly until he was very nearly certain.

Perhaps someone had been assigned to watch over him, to provide protection. That idea he promptly dismissed; he was hardly the sort of person to receive such attention in a communist nation. In fact Mark Day had too often made things very difficult for the agents of such powers.

It could be the people that Morgan had mentioned, that was more likely. In fact it was quite likely indeed, though how they had been positioned so fast he could not imagine. Probably it was only one person; more than that would be unnecessary.

If this explanation was not correct, then he might have a problem on his hands. Carefully he flexed his fingers, closing them into fists and then opening them up again as though he were tuning them for some possible action. One thing was going for him: few people would expect that middle-aged, nonathletic Edwin Nesbitt, who went about his business quietly, had made a hobby of the Japanese martial arts and was moderately proficient in their use. One man had found that out in Berlin: perhaps he had passed the information along to others.

Nesbitt began to plan his actions. He could go straight back to his hotel and use it as a haven, but it was now many blocks away and on the other side of the central square. Even at a sudden brisk walk, which would be dangerous in itself, it would take him a minimum of fifteen minutes to get there.

Plus which running away was usually a most ineffective way of dealing with any situation.

Mark Day would know what to do, of course. He was well-schooled in all of the tricks of the trade, plus which he had several more of his own. Better than the old dodge of bending over to tie a shoelace, especially since Nesbitt had not worn laced shoes for years.

As he thought he walked on, pacing himself so that he would not give away his knowledge that he was not alone. He could turn a corner and duck into a doorway, but the best that that maneuver could do would be to bring him face to face with his unseen companion. That might be the last thing he would want.

He could try to lose the man, but how? The inventiveness that served him so well in his study at home had nothing immediate to suggest. Then a very simple thought came to him: why not let Mark Day take over.

In the centuries-old city that had seen and had hidden so much, the man from the secret Washington bureau walked calmly. He had no fear; he had met this same situation many times and he knew what to do. He was aware that he was being followed, that was the essential thing, and whoever was behind him did not know that he knew. To preserve that advantage Day strolled on exactly as before, apparently deep in his own thoughts. But as he did so his alert eyes missed no detail of the street and he listened for any sound that would tell him more.

Underneath the beautifully tailored Italian suit that he was wearing his trained muscles were fully at his command, but he was not tense. A sudden bullet in the back might cut him down, but if his shadow had any such intentions, he would have to come much closer to use a hand gun effectively. It was most unlikely that he would be armed with anything more deadly.

As he came up to the next intersection Mark glanced each way as any casual sightseer would do, but in that brief interval his mind photographed with remarkable accuracy the contents of the cross street in both directions. Based on what he had seen, he made a quick, careful decision to cross and turn right. It would make him a standout target for a few seconds, but the position of the lone streetlamp was in his favor if he stayed out of the cone of its direct light.

He wheeled abruptly as though he had just made up his mind and walked a little faster than before — the natural actions of a man who had just decided to return to his hotel. In three timed breaths he reached the opposite curb; before he had drawn another into his lungs he was safely behind the corner of a massive stone building and, he knew, for probably close to half a minute out of sight of the person behind him.

Immediately he began to run, silently, swiftly — ready now to make his move. His first glance had told him that the second huge structure, also of stone, had recessed dark doorways and as an added architectural feature several small false balconies in front of its second-story windows. What was even more to the point, the trim design around the doorways was of slightly protruding heavy quoins —

*they extended out a scant two inches, but that was enough
to provide a good foothold.*

*When he was halfway past the face of the second build-
ing he knew that he had pushed his luck far enough: the
time remaining to him could not be more than a scant few
seconds. His breathing still controlled despite his exertions,
Mark Day reached the doorway and without any waste
motion climbed swiftly upward. He was careful to do so on
the far side of the balcony so that he would have the additional screening if it was needed. He reached the balcony
in seven seconds, vaulted over the low railing and flung
himself flat. Less than three seconds later he saw the figure
of a man come around the corner and begin to make his
way toward him. The man stayed very close to the side of
the building and remained in heavy shadow. If he made any
sound whatever, Day could not hear it from where he lay.*

*Quickly and calmly Mark took stock. His shadow could
be and probably was hostile, but there was a chance that he
was one of Morgan's people. Before long he would pass
directly under the balcony on which he himself lay. It might
be a simple thing to drop directly onto his back, but there
were good reasons why it should not be done. If the man
below, or his superiors, had the proper connections, it
could be very uncomfortable for Day — this was, after all,
Prague and behind the Iron Curtain. Explanations would
be required as to why Day was there and if the answers
were not satisfactory, there could be another of those ses-
sions in a secret cellar that would be very unpleasant
indeed.*

*It was the better part of valor, Mark decided, just to dis-
appear. If his hiding place was discovered, then he would*

63

take appropriate action and he would still have the advantage of attacking from above.

As his shadower came silently down the street, pausing with exquisite caution just before each darkened doorway, the man he was stalking lay perfectly still, breathing easily, with his cheek on the narrow stone that was supporting him in order to keep the lowest possible profile. He did not look up, trusting entirely to his ears to keep him informed.

He could see the luminous dial of his watch and read the progress of the sweep second hand. Based on what he had observed, he timed in his mind the progress of the man below him and when his follower should have been close by, he listened with utmost concentration. He was rewarded; the four separate sounds that he heard were all remarkably minute and so brief that he could not identify any of them, but they told him all that he needed to know. His pursuer was directly below him and he was a professional.

Ninety seconds later by his watch Day lifted his head very slowly and looked through the balustrade. His shadow was almost at the end of the block and walking faster. Then, abruptly, he stopped and waited. Mark had expected that, but he lay in a dark enough shadow to risk keeping his head up to see what was going on; it would be much more dangerous not to know.

The man stood near to the corner, his back close against a building and remaining still. For almost five minutes he did not move; then almost like a phantom he disappeared. Mark's muscles were beginning to protest their cramped position, but he could do nothing to relieve them completely. He did shift his position a little so that he could watch both ends of the block with a simple turning of his head.

His guess was right, the man who had been following him appeared silently and almost invisibly at the opposite end of the street, having gone around the block in the matter of a minute or two. Once more the shadower retraced his original steps, obviously giving fresh attention to every detail. Mark knew that he could tumble to the balcony trick at any moment, the only reason that he had not done so was probably because he believed that he had been tailing an inept amateur who had no reason to suspect anything.

From one of the darkened doorways there was a noise. Not a loud one, but a scraping that might have betrayed an accidental movement. The man below reacted almost instantly; within a second or two he was in a deep shadow area at the intersection of two buildings, but not before Mark had seen him slip his hand inside his coat. It was still for half a minute, then a prowling cat emerged from where the sound had been and made its silent way down the sidewalk.

That slight incident seemed to affect Day's pursuer; when he appeared once more he walked a trifle faster. For the second time he passed directly underneath his quarry without detecting Mark's presence and continued on down the street. In less than three minutes he reached the end of the next block and disappeared.

When he was back down on the pavement once more, Ed Nesbitt brushed off his suit as best he could and then continued his walk back toward the hotel. Nothing else happened to impede his progress; although he remained watchful, he did not detect anything unusual at all during the time that it took him to reach his destination. He entered the lobby quite openly and asked for his case and key.

Perhaps, just perhaps, the clerk who handed them to him seemed slightly surprised, but it was a vague impression at the best. Nesbitt went upstairs and found his room apparently exactly as he had left it. A check of the attaché case told him that no exchange had been made — he still had the one he had been handed at Frankfurt. He locked the door as he usually did, shot the bolt, and went to bed.

5

AT NINE the following morning Josef appeared at the hotel in time to intercept Nesbitt during the early stages of his breakfast; Ed invited the younger man to join him and after a certain suitable display of reluctance, the offer was accepted. Another look at the wretched quality of the suit that Josef was attempting to wear so bravely convinced him that his hospitality was not being misplaced; he doubted if the young Czech had had a good square meal all month.

While they were eating they discussed the publishing firm and its plans for the future insofar as the Mark Day stories were concerned. "They are tremendously good," Josef declared with conviction, "and we are immensely proud to offer them here." He lowered his voice. "There are certain political considerations, you will understand, that require us either to make a few changes, or, if that cannot be done effectively, to pass certain of your books by entirely. Believe me, this is not our wish — but I think that you understand."

It struck Nesbitt that the young man was trying his utmost to be a good representative of the publishing house despite the fact that the salary he received had to be minimal. His eagerness was apparent and his ability to speak English outstanding.

After he had finished his second cup of somewhat bitter coffee, Ed arose and announced that he was ready to pay the call that was his official excuse for visiting the city. Josef had a small and drastically underpowered Czech-built car waiting; Nesbitt folded up inside and allowed himself to be taken to his destination. By the way that his guide was driving he deduced that the car was not his own — he had a certain jerkiness on the controls and when they had first started, there had been a moment's unfamiliarity with the ignition lock. That had provided all of the evidence that was necessary.

The offices of the publishing company proved to be in a very small suite located in a building that had been standing for an indefinite period of time. It was evident that certain preparations had been made for the visit of a best-selling American author; the telltale indications of an unusual cleanup could be read and there was coffee ready and waiting. The cracked cups had been carefully washed and the sugar container had been freshly filled.

The managing director who came forward to greet Nesbitt was somewhere in his fifties. As he held out his hand the warmth of his greeting overrode the fact that he was not of prepossessing appearance. He was of only medium stature, if that, and wore a pair of glasses that was not well fitted to his features, the narrow black rims contrasting with the thin frizzle of mouse-colored hair that baldness had not yet swept away. The clothing he wore was hardly better than Josef's, but it fitted the setting of close-to-worn-out furniture and the general feeling that nothing new would be added to the office furnishings for some time to come. The firm was alive, but it was hardly prospering. However, it was his publisher, or one of them, and Nesbitt did his best to play the part of a genuinely interested guest.

"Mr. Nesbitt, it is such an honor having you here in person," the director began, and Nesbitt knew at once that the little speech had been carefully rehearsed. "Please sit down. Will you have some coffee?"

Without waiting for an answer the single office girl, whose appearance had been improved as much as possible for the occasion, poured out three cups. She served them with proper protocol mixed with a modest percentage of feminine style. Poor girl, Nesbitt thought, she had a right to be noticed. He thanked her in a way that suggested his mild interest and was rewarded with a smile that made the girl almost radiant.

The director continued, speaking English that was labored and difficult for him, but which showed the evidence of careful study.

"I shall not ask you to pronounce my name, it is too difficult," he began. "My first name is Anton which I invite you to use."

"Ed," Nesbitt said.

"Very good." The director paused and then gathered himself for an additional effort. "We have, as you know, political problems in the conduct of our business. Please do not discuss this, but we are under controls — we dare not displease certain people."

"I'm quite aware of the situation," Nesbitt said. "Some of my books treat communist regimes in a manner they don't always appreciate."

"That is true," the director agreed. "Also they are, I think, perhaps the best. It is for us difficult that we publish you at all, it is allowed because it is window trimming — it suggests a freedom we do not have."

Nesbitt remained silent, realizing the difficulty his host was having with a language he spoke very infrequently.

"Mr. Ed," the director went on, "we have funds for you. They are in crowns, of course." He spread his hands with visible eloquence. "You cannot take any of them with you out of the country, it is forbidden. But you may spend them here."

"I don't have much time," Nesbitt said.

"If you wish, Josef will help you, we have the car for the full day. In Prague we have fine leather goods; also our crystal is very fine. Some is for sale in hard currencies only, but there are many pieces that crowns will buy."

"I can use some of them to pay my hotel bill."

The director hesitated for a fraction of a moment, it was so slight that Nesbitt almost missed it. "We shall take care of that," he said.

"No," Nesbitt countered. "I always insist on paying my own charges." He read a quick reaction and added to his declaration. "It is much better for me that way because of the American income tax."

70

"If you insist, but we. . . ." Instead of finishing the sentence he opened the flat middle drawer of his desk and took out an envelope which he handed over. Nesbitt looked inside it and saw a considerable number of bills — he could not evaluate their worth.

The director read his mind. "In United States dollars it is almost three thousand," he said.

It was all clear to Nesbitt then — the small publishing firm that struggled along, but it dealt honorably with its authors as far as the authorities would let it. He had no way of checking the amount, but it was enough money to convince him of their fairness. He thought rapidly and then made a decision he knew he would not regret — he had no idea when he would be in Prague again.

"I'll probably spend some of this," he said, "but certainly not all. I'd like to leave the rest with you. My suggestion is that you use it for the firm's general purposes until I come back — or the regulations change. I don't like money to be idle when it can be of some use."

The moment that he had finished speaking he could detect a change in the atmosphere. They had known that he was coming for weeks — and God only knew how much they had probably sacrificed to put that package of cash together for him. It was relief that he sensed, an unexpected reprieve that none of the other three persons present betrayed, but it was there nonetheless.

"Under the regulations, I do not know how I can give you security," the director said.

"I don't require it," Nesbitt told him. "Let's say that I'm unofficially investing in the business. Don't put anything down on paper; we know each other and that's sufficient."

It was a minimal sacrifice because he could not possibly

71

spend three thousand dollars in one day and he had no choice but to leave whatever remained behind him. It would probably be safer in his publisher's hands than anywhere else he could think of, plus which it might do some good in his absence.

"You are too generous," Anton responded. "We shall do our best to deserve your trust." He turned toward the office girl. "I forget my manners. Mr. Nesbitt, my daughter Marla."

Ed stood up and shook hands. He was about to say something about getting a new typewriter, the ancient machine on Marla's desk looked hopelessly cumbersome, when he realized how tactless that would be — he was not there to criticize the office appointments.

Anton stood up also. "I shall send you your sales reports regularly," he promised. "Now I suggest that you see something more of our city. Some people have said that it is like the setting of a fairy tale."

"I can believe that," Nesbitt replied, "only you have too many wicked witches. I'm going out on a ten o'clock flight tonight, but could we have an early dinner together?"

"Of course, you honor us. But please, you be our guest. On this I insist."

It made no real difference, of course, so Nesbitt consented. "All right, Josef can phone in later for the time and place."

During the rest of the morning he went with Josef to some of the shops of Prague. He bought himself a good quality suede leather jacket for which he had a real use. Later, at the crystal showrooms where his crowns were good for only a small portion of the products on display, he selected an exquisite hand-cut vase and a set of cocktail glasses. After the problem of shipping had been resolved, Nesbitt declined to do any more shopping. "There isn't anything else that I want," he declared, "I'd rather see more of the city."

From the hilltop crowned by the magnificent cathedral of St. Vitus he stood with his guide drinking in the long view of the ancient capital and letting the sensation of its reality sink into his being. He watched the majestic Moldau and thought of the magnificent music of Smetana. It was all beauty and antiquity from where he stood and the sordid ravages of politics were mercifully invisible. The feeling stayed with him even while Josef pointed out the former palace and reminded him how, in 1618, the infamous Defenestrations of Prague had taken place there. He visualized the scene as the imperial counselors had been physically thrown from the windows to inaugurate the Thirty Years' War; the city that lay stretched out before and below him was like the stuff of dreams and his fingers itched for the keys of a typewriter to record it all while it was in the forefront of his mind.

When he at last turned away the feeling stayed with him, even while they were touring the inside of the vast church. It was renewed when he visited the street of the goldsmiths, the row of tightly packed little houses and shops where the alchemists had been housed and provided for while they carried on their endless efforts to convert base metals into gold.

In the bright light of a pleasant day he was taken also to see underground cells shaped like beehives with the only means of exit located at the center top of the roof; from here prisoners could be let down into the dark round windowless holes from which no escape was possible and there was nothing to look at but the locked grilling far out of reach overhead. He saw also fireplaces so constructed that there were short passageways behind them and coffin-like chambers where unfortunate prisoners could be sealed upright to be baked alive.

Charm and savagery — the indivisible heritage of the once medieval city — made Nesbitt set his jaw and file it all away for use in the near future. There were many many secrets in this ancient capital too — and in every other one of similar longevity throughout the world. From this combination, and the fact that it persisted into the present day, he made his living.

In the long rectangular center of Prague Josef drove slowly while he pointed out verbally the bullet and shell holes in the ancient buildings that had been left there by the Russian invasion and spoke of the thunder of mighty tanks that had come when Czechoslovakia had dared to reach for a bit of freedom. When the car had cleared the central area, Josef tightened his fingers on the wheel. "Mr. Nesbitt," he said. "May I speak with you?"

"Of course."

"Mr. Nesbitt, I have no right to do this, but I ask for your help."

Ed thought of the money still bulging the envelope in his pocket and did not wonder that the underpaid clerk hoped to borrow some of it. "Go ahead," he invited.

Josef scanned the area as if to assure himself that no one was observing them too closely. "We want to get out," he said. "Marla and I. She is my wife. Life here — I cannot describe it to you. We cannot even think to ourselves for fear that we will show it in some way."

"I didn't believe it was that bad in Czechoslovakia," Nesbitt commented.

"Sir, you do not live here. We have talked it over with my father-in-law and he will help us in every way that he can. He too would like to come out, but he is too old to find a place somewhere else. And he has no great skills that your world would want to have."

"What would he do without you and Marla?"

"He will manage, he has told us that. He will say that he knew nothing of our plans and that by leaving, if we can get away, we have ruined his business."

Because he did not know what he should say, Nesbitt remained quiet.

"If we can succeed," Josef went on, "then we will try to send for him. It is already understood."

"What can I do?" Ed asked.

"I only ask that if things can be arranged, that you offer to sponsor us. It will cost you nothing, we will see to that. It may be enough to get us out of the country; once we are free, we will be able to take care of ourselves."

"You are planning to live in the United States then?"

Josef shook his head. "No, that is too much to hope. If we can only get to Vienna, then from there it will not be difficult at all to reach Israel. For us that is the homeland."

"You have my address," Nesbitt said. "When you are ready, write to me and I will do the best that I can. It won't be necessary to put down exactly what you mean — I can read between the lines."

"Sir — I thank you! If for any reason money is needed, we will pay it back to you. On this I give you my word."

He dropped his voice despite the fact that there was no

75

one to hear outside the car. "I know, Mr. Nesbitt, that you are more than just an author. It is very important what you write, yes, but I have read all of your books and I know. You are also with the U.S. Government — that is why I ask you for help. We trust you."

There was no point in denying anything, because he would not be believed. Knowing that, Nesbitt let it pass. "I'll do whatever I can," he promised once more.

"Thank you, sir, thank you," Josef said just loud enough to be heard. "And Mr. Nesbitt, I know how you hid on the balcony when they were following you. That is how I know who you really are."

Ed was suddenly very alert indeed. "Where were you?" he asked.

"Do not ask me that. I only tell you that there are some who would protect you. When you went out from your hotel last night, they watched. When it was discovered that you were being followed, they made it their business to see that you were not alone in this city. That could be very dangerous. But you required no help. That is how we know that you are really not Mr. Nesbitt, you are Mark Day."

The train ride, which had promised so much, turned out to be a minor disaster. The coaches were crowded to the point where standees were everywhere. The cars were dirty and badly maintained. Most of the passengers seemed to be surrounded by crying babies and orange peelings on the floor; there was absolutely no emotional magic whatever to be found, none of the glamour that went automatically with the name of the Orient Express.

The inconvenience and partial discomfort did not bother Nesbitt, he could take it as it came, but to find that the Orient Express was a prosaic, overcrowded, totally unromantic, and somewhat smelly string of strictly functional cars was a bitter disillusionment. He concluded that there were no spies on the train for the very good reason that there wasn't room for any. He sat, in supposed first class comfort, in an aisle seat farthest removed from the window in the company of five others who were intent on their own affairs. The wooden-faced girl who had the choice window seat facing forward had pulled the curtain down three quarters of the way to spare herself the view, and in so doing had denied both the man in the middle seat and Nesbitt any opportunity to glimpse anything along the way.

The others in the compartment, even after searching inspection by Nesbitt, offered nothing whatever in the way of a possible story lead. No one wished to talk to him. For a while he took his attaché case onto his lap and tried to work, but the jouncing of the train made the attempt all but totally futile. Because he could do nothing about it, he accepted his fate and clung to the thought that it would not be too much longer until he was in Venice.

Sometime in the afternoon the train at last pulled slowly into a long shed and came to a stop. Venice was announced. Glad to have the disappointing experience behind him, Nesbitt got off wondering if it had been a mistake to come here at all. Perhaps it would have been best to leave Venice to Edgar Allen Poe; the mundane nature of the long train platform was certainly not inspiring.

"Mr. Nesbitt?"

He turned to find just what he expected, the stereotype European transfer man and guide who was there to meet him.

"Welcome to Venice, Mr. Nesbitt. Let me take your case for you." The man almost grabbed it out of his hand.

At that moment Nesbitt realized that his mood was considerably fouler than he had allowed for. He had been looking forward to the Orient Express as one of the highlights of his trip and it had bombed out completely. He had not even been allowed to look out the window to study the countryside, which was one of the techniques he used constantly. Then, on top of all that, his first look at Venice was about as exciting as the Cleveland City Dump.

He forced himself to be reasonable. "I'll keep my case, if you don't mind, but perhaps you can arrange for my bags."

"Of course, sir, I'll be glad to. May I be shown which ones they are?"

As Nesbitt pointed them out he took a fresh hold on himself, then as he started down the long platform toward the exit with his guide and a porter bringing up the rear, he did some inward soul-searching.

"Look," he told himself as clearly as any line of dialogue he had ever written. "The whole business that you're in is an illusion. There are spies, of course, but it's a dirty business and the people who are in it are after the money and that's all. Except for a few dedicated individuals, and you haven't a chance in hell of meeting any of them. The whole world of Mark Day doesn't exist, so don't keep trying to find it in reality. Be content to get your background data and then go home and spin your romantic webs. But don't fall for your own literary confections."

They reached the gate and passed through. "I have a taxi waiting, sir," the guide said. He led the way down a few broad steps to the end. Nesbitt looked, and the doors of his mind swung open. It was not a street, it was a canal. There were others he could see as well, and the taxi that awaited him was sleekly bobbing in the water.

As Nesbitt climbed on board his spirits were already much improved. As soon as he was seated in the stern the baggage was passed on board and the taxi cast off. It was not a long ride, but he enjoyed every moment of it, especially when the taxi emerged from the rather narrow waterway onto a great curving wide expanse that could only be the Grand Canal. This was Venice as he had imagined it: the ancient buildings rising vertically out of the water as they had when the Doges had ruled this unique city.

The taxi entered a narrower canal, turned into yet another, and then drew up before a landing stage where a doorman and a bellhop stood waiting.

The moment that he was in the lobby Nesbitt knew that this was a hotel in the fine European tradition of genuine elegance. He did not care for pretentions, but this hostelry needed none; it was the genuine thing. Unquestionably Mark Day would stay here, unless his assignment required him to hide out in much more modest surroundings.

With a growing sense of well-being, Nesbitt stepped to the counter to register. As would be expected, the clerk spoke excellent English and knew at once which language to use. "Good afternoon, sir," he greeted. "Welcome to the Bauer Gruenwald. We are most honored to have you stopping here." He completed the formalities of the registration and then spoke again. "After you have had a chance to refresh yourself, Mr. Nesbitt, you might wish to take tea on the terrace."

Nesbitt signed a traveler's check and passed it over. "I think I'll just rest for a bit," he said.

The clerk accepted the check and handed it to a colleague to be cashed. "If you will allow me, sir, you might wish to inspect it while your luggage is being taken upstairs."

At that moment Nesbitt recalled the many times that Mark Day had been supplied with a vital bit of information, very seldom in as clear a manner as that. He wondered if they thought he was an idiot, then he realized that he had already turned down the first suggestion. Maybe they were right. "Perhaps I will," he answered. "You will take care of everything for me?"

"Absolutely, sir. Here are your funds. There is a gentlemen's room right over there, sir, if you require it to freshen up."

That made the situation even clearer. He accepted the lire handed to him and pushed back a bill for the bellhop. Then he went to the washroom and repaired some of the damage his appearance had sustained on the long train ride. As he recombed his hair the mirror told him that he was about at par, which would have to do. He picked up his case, which he made it a point always to carry now, and presently walked down the long corridor toward the refreshment terrace at the end.

As he stepped out onto the open area he was faced by a sweeping panorama of Venice with the Grand Canal almost at his feet. It was superb and he took a deep breath to drink it all in. The Orient Express had been a fiasco, but this was Venice in all of the magnificence that he had envisioned. With a lighter step he began to weave his way through the empty tables toward those closer to the water's edge that were occupied. And there, as expected and looking what must have been very close to her best, was Celestine Van Damm.

She was watching as he approached, her smile belying the fact that he was only plain Ed Nesbitt who had been denied even a fraction of the compelling good looks that Mark Day possessed. He did not walk with the easy, controlled strides that marked his fictional hero. Doing the best that he could, he stood across from her for a brief moment before he spoke. Since he could not think of anything brilliant to say, he contented himself with the obvious. "Good afternoon," he offered.

He received an even more stunning welcoming smile, and a gesture toward a chair at her side. "I've been expecting you," she said. "Please sit down, Mr. Day."

"I'm not Mark Day," Nesbitt declared after he had ordered. "I wish to hell that I could be, but it isn't in me."

"I'm not so sure," Celestine responded.

"I am." He decided to go on without allowing himself to think about it. "I'll make a confession, if you'd like. Once, in a very foolish moment, I offered my services to . . . . a branch of the government. They all but laughed at me. I guess because I write fiction, they thought that was all that I could do."

Celestine rested her chin on her hand while she surveyed him. "I already know you better than that. Also, did you know that in England they called up most of their good authors during the war years for intelligence duty?"

"I heard about it." He did not trust himself to say more.

"Enough of that." Celestine raised her head and looked out for a moment at the spectacle of Venice. As she did so her well-formed breasts were sharply outlined and Nesbitt admired them with full appreciation. "What are you planning for the rest of the day?" she asked.

"I'd like to look around Venice a bit and see St. Mark's square; I've heard so much about it."

"Why not," Celestine said. "It's very close by, we can walk it in five minutes."

This time Ed was a little faster on the uptake. "Then, later, perhaps we could find a nice place to have some dinner."

Celestine sipped her coffee. "I'd like that. Tell me — what's in your case? I noticed that you always carry it."

"All of my notes, for one thing. They're very important to me. My travel documents and some other things I wouldn't want to lose."

"Then it's best to keep it with you." She left it at that. "After we finish our coffee, give me a few minutes and I'll meet you in the lobby."

While he was putting on a fresh shirt Ed reviewed the matter in his mind. Celestine Van Damm! Dammit, he had created that girl out of whole ectoplasm, or so he had thought; now here she was in the living flesh — and hellishly attractive flesh at that. He didn't understand it — but he didn't understand a lot of the things that had been happening to him lately. Gretel Hoffmeister, the phony reporter. George Smith who was "with the government" and who had promised to keep him in sight. The episode of being followed in Prague. He tied his tie without having reached a conclusion about anything.

In the lobby he noted something: the whole visible staff seemed to take it for granted that Celestine was specifically his, and apparently thought nothing of it at all. He remembered once more that he was in Europe, specifically in Italy, and that the Italians had never been observed to be backward in matters where romance was concerned. This wasn't a romance, but if they chose to consider it one, he had no serious objections.

His opinion was reinforced when Celestine reappeared. She had changed, as any woman would, and was as freshly inviting as though fatigue had never touched her. In the company of this fascinating young female Nesbitt went out the side door onto the streets of Venice, and was at once surrounded with the realization that they were all that he had hoped they would be. They were narrow by ordinary standards because they carried no vehicular traffic, but they were quite wide enough for comfortable walking in the spotted sunlight that slanted out of the clear Italian sky. On both sides there was a continuous series of shops that displayed jewelry, wonderful Venetian glass, and other inviting wares that seemed in themselves part of the Venice of history and legend — the place where every form of human passion and endeavor had passed across the stage and was passing still.

It was all accentuated by the fact that the girl beside him was too real to be believed. He thought of her as a girl, but she had matured beyond that into a woman with all the latent capabilities that potent word implied. Thirty, perhaps, but he did not really care. She was still young, but experienced enough to be vastly more desirable to him than the dewy twenty-year-olds who populated the marriage block in the society columns. He stole another look at her and realized that his masculine instincts were being aroused. So this was the creature that Mark Day took to bed with him! She was fully a match for him, and that was as strong an endorsement as he could give.

"Here we are," she said.

He took his attention away from her to look before him and saw it almost exactly as he had imagined it in his mind — the Piazza San Marco. It was all there, the long distorted rectangle of pavement with its hoards of pigeons, the chairs scattered about in front of various establishments, the famous bell tower, and at the far end the Basilica of St. Mark with its four great bronze horses high above the doorway.

It was full of people, but that did not distract him. As he walked out onto the main area he was content to be one of the many, becoming for a moment part of the life of the ancient, unique city. From a street peddler he bought some cracked corn and fed the pigeons like any tourist. So did Celestine, and as the birds swarmed over her, he felt a quick, almost savage sense of possession. He hardly knew her in person, but he had lived with her through many books and that made her part of him.

He took his time, walking around the square until he could obtain the best view from the ground of the Moors on the Clock Tower, the timeless ringers who had been cast in the fifteenth century, five years after Christopher Columbus had first set foot onto the New World. Nesbitt made his living by creating the atmosphere in which his characters lived and breathed; now he let the rich and full miasma of this incomparable place sink into his consciousness until he had it fully imprinted on his memory for years to come.

"If you'd like to walk just a block down toward the water, we can see the Bridge of Sighs," Celestine told him.

He liked the way she had put that, foregoing her obvious knowledge of the city in order to play the role of a first time sightseer with him. Not too many women would be that intelligent and he knew it. "By all means," he answered.

A few minutes later they stood together on a small bridge over a narrow canal directly off the main St. Mark's basin, looking at the famous landmark which owed its celebrity to the fact that it connected the doge's palace with the adjacent prison. On the water below one of the inevitable black gondolas made the classic picture complete. Nesbitt took in the scene, filed it away in his mind, and then was ready to move on. "What do you suggest now?" he asked.

"We could take one of the walks along the canals, the *fondemente*. They're quite interesting."

"Good. Lead the way, will you?"

As they went back across the square Nesbitt had an odd reaction: this was Mark Day's girl, so what right did he have to be in her company? He almost expected Day himself to appear at any moment to reclaim his own, after which Mark and Celestine would be off on another of their mad whirls which invariably ended up in the warm confines of a soft European bed.

With an effort he reminded himself that there was no Mark Day, but it was harder than usual, because here beside him, and very much alive, was the also supposedly fictional Celestine. That forced him to consider her for a moment as a sexual partner for himself. It was a dazzling prospect, but he forced it out of his mind — not because of any misplaced moral sense, but because he knew that he simply wasn't in that league.

Mark Day was a superman and for him, and the life he had chosen to live, there were certain exceptional compensations. Ed had planned it that way and judging by the sales figures, it had worked out very well. In such company he was a stranger, he knew it, and he had been wise enough never to intrude.

Five minutes after they had left the square the scene had almost drastically changed. The spaciousness of the plaza had given way to a narrow, deeply shadowed corridor between ancient buildings. Most of it was filled with dark and featureless water, but there was a walkway that was quite sufficient for the two of them. Celestine slipped her hand through his arm and they were for the moment very close together.

In contrast to the milling crowd in the square they were almost alone. When he heard footsteps Nesbitt glanced back, but it was nothing but a young man in a knit T-shirt apparently immersed in his own thoughts. A water taxi, its engine echoing from the close walls, came leisurely down toward them; when the boatman looked up, Ed shook his head. Still the boatman tried, he guided his craft closer and raised his hat in invitation.

Abruptly and without warning, Nesbitt felt his case being snatched from his grasp. He tried at once to tighten his hold, but it was already too late. When he sought to whirl, he could not because Celestine was still holding onto his right arm.

"*Hey!*" he yelled.

He could have saved himself that futile effort. The young man in the T-shirt ran three quick steps and then jumped lightly and expertly into the back of the slow-moving boat. The moment that he hit, the boatman shoved the throttle forward, the engine roared with fresh power, and a wake sprang up at the boat's stern. In helpless frustration Nesbitt saw the boat rapidly retreat down the canal, the young man taunting him by waving the attaché case above his head. Presently the boat slowed, managed a sharp corner into another canal, and disappeared.

Rage, frustration, and humiliation surged through Nesbitt until he could hardly control himself. It had all been very neatly done, and like a backwoods simpleton he had simply stood there and let it happen! And that case was probably much more precious than the thieves would ever know.

Blind with anger, he swore aloud and cursed his own ineptness. In another ten minutes, his good sense told him, the identifying sticker would be off the case and recovery would be impossible. He had been successfully played for a first-class idiot and his fledgling career as an intelligence courier was abruptly over.

6

"WE MUST call the police," Celestine said.

"A fat lot of good that will do," Nesbitt retorted. His mind was still revolting against what had so recently happened.

Celestine understood. "I know, but we must try anyway. There should be a phone somewhere near here."

"Do you speak Italian?" Nesbitt asked.

"Enough, I think."

He had never felt more impotent in his life. His nerves grated during the next five minutes while they located a small shopping area; once there Celestine had no difficulty in finding a public phone. While she was making the call he took savage revenge on himself by sketching the scene in his mind as if Mark Day himself had actually been there.

As the thief snatched the case from Mark's hand, he jerked away and ran three fast steps toward the boat. Celestine was still clinging to Day's arm, and because in sudden fright she had tightened her grasp, it took almost a whole second for the American agent to free himself without hurting her.

By that time the engine of the boat was already beginning to pick up its tempo. The man holding Day's case jumped, timing himself to land as close to the center of the decking as he could. He was so sure of himself he did not attempt to look back after he had hit on the balls of his feet and had steadied himself.

With the honed reflexes of the professional athlete, Mark was already in close pursuit. He did not waste any precious breath in calling out — it would have been ridiculous; instead he gulped air at precisely the right moment and flung himself forward. His right foot hit the very edge of the pavement and from there he jumped. His taut body arced through the air; then he landed solidly on the last two feet of the stern. It was all that he needed; his forward momentum gave him his balance and he was ready for action.

Warned, the thief dropped the case containing the vital microfilm and whipped himself around. He attempted to reach under his clothing for the knife he had concealed, but his time had run out. Day seized him by the arm, whirled, and sent him, arms and legs outstretched, over the side. He made a lazy quarter-turn in the air before he landed face-first in prone position on the water. The splash he made was spectacular, but Mark did not see it. He used the time instead to reach the boatman in two swift strikes. He seized the man around the upper arms in a steel grip and with a sidewise jerk snapped his head hard against the side structure of the cockpit.

The boatman let out an animal yelp of agony that testified to his pain and his submission — he wanted no more treatment like that. Taking no unnecessary chances, Day slid his hand into his pocket to suggest that he had a weapon there. "Now," he snapped, "as soon as you feel well enough, you can take me where I tell you to go."

Celestine came back. "We've been asked to return to the hotel," she reported, "the police will be contacting us there shortly."

Feeling a complete fool, and made more so because he was in the company of a girl he would have preferred to have impressed favorably, Nesbitt started back with her toward the Bauer Gruenwald. On the way he considered the impact of the outrage he had just sustained. All of his travel documents except his passport had been in the case. All of the notes he had taken en route; material that was essential to his work. His traveler's checks could be replaced, but it was an inconvenient business at best. The case had also contained certain letters of introduction that were important. And, in addition to everything else, it was a rather special case in itself.

The case!

It had been planted on him in Frankfurt, now it had been snatched away again. There was a good chance that the two events were related, but why make him the dummy just to go from Frankfurt to Venice? It didn't make sense.

Celestine sensed his mood fully, but for the first time in nine books she said the wrong thing. "Don't blame yourself, Mark Day himself couldn't have done any better."

Nesbitt tightened, he couldn't help it, then Celestine returned to her usual form. "I feel so guilty," she added. "I was hanging on to you like death; I should have had sense enough not to tie you up like that."

What a helluva woman she was! "Right now," he told her, "I'd rather go to bed with you than with any female who ever drew breath." He knew she would understand.

"Let's get your case back first," she suggested.

When they reached the lobby of the hotel he turned to Celestine. "What's your room number?" he asked.

"I'm right next to you, didn't you know?"

He hadn't known and his first thought was to wonder if there would be a connecting door. It was only an academic notion, he was too concerned with his loss to dwell on it as he rode with her up the elevator. As soon as he was in his own room he had a compelling urge for a shower. The police were coming, but probably not during the next eight or nine minutes. He stripped down and allowed his spirits to recuperate as the water gushed over his body, washing away some of his travel weariness and with it part of his sense of guilt. For a little while he had actually allowed himself the impossible dream that in some small way he could fulfill the role of Mark Day — there had been the incident of the hotel thief in Berlin. But his ineptness in allowing his case to be taken away from him so easily was an ugly reality he could not dismiss or explain away.

The phone rang while he was drying off. "Are you decent?" Celestine asked.

"Of course. I'm also stark naked."

"I'll come right in."

"Fine," he told her, "just be sure you're the same way."

He finished with the towel and enjoyed the luxury of clean linen. He was stepping into a pair of presentable slacks when the phone rang once more. This time it was the desk downstairs. "Inspector Franzini is here to see you, sir."

An inspector! He had expected a sergeant at the most; tourists must always be losing things in this mind-distracting city. "Ask him if he would care to come up," he said.

He had time to put a shirt on and get it properly adjusted before there was a tap on his door. He opened it to admit a man who was instantly ready to step into the pages of his next book. The inspector was perhaps forty, but his age was meaningless in view of his faultless grooming and an urbane air which marked him a continental gentleman of unquestioned status. Nesbitt's immediate reaction was that he did not have a police problem worthy of a man of this stature; he welcomed his guest into the room, asked him to sit down, and suggested refreshment.

The inspector seated himself with accomplished ease, declined anything to eat or drink, and then consumed only a few seconds in glancing about the room. "My name is Franzini," he said in excellent English. "I am most delighted to meet such a famous guest to our city. May I hope that I shall be presented to the fascinating Miss Van Damm?"

Nesbitt reached for the phone. "I'll ask her to come over," he stated.

The inspector raised a hand. "Perhaps we could have a private word together first?"

"Of course."

"This is your first trip to Venice, I believe."

"That's correct."

"Do you have any friends or acquaintances in the city?"

"No — none whatever."

"Any enemies, perhaps? Applying the word very broadly."

"I don't know anyone here at all."

The inspector settled back. "Since you arrived only this afternoon, it would appear that someone has very good sources of information and also the ability to organize things quickly."

"Excuse me, inspector," Nesbitt said, "but I don't believe that's the case. You see there was no way that anyone could have anticipated where Miss Van Damm and I were going. It seems much more likely that the thief and his boatman accomplice were looking for a mark and they found one. Me."

"That is very logical," the inspector agreed. "But there are also certain other considerations. Please be kind enough to tell me exactly what happened as fully as you can."

Nesbitt obliged. Because he was a good reporter his account was lucid, concise, and accurate. In giving it he did not neglect what he still considered to be his own stupidity in falling such an easy victim.

Franzini listened with every sign of close attention. When the recital was finished he produced a map of Venice and spread it out. "I realize that you do not know

93

our city as yet," he said, "but perhaps you can give me some idea where this occurred."

Nesbitt could do much better than that. With the aid of the map he was able to retrace the movements of Celestine and himself and point out the exact place where the theft of his attaché case had taken place. The inspector was impressed with his ability to recall and said so. "Now, if you please," he continued, "the exact contents of your briefcase."

As Nesbitt listed them Franzini took notes and nodded his approval once more when the inventory had been completed. "I do not wonder that you are such a successful novelist," he declared. "You visualize things so very clearly. It is a great help, of course." He paused and deliberately took his time. "Now as to the case itself," he said at last, "is it in any way unusual?"

Nesbitt shook his head. "Unfortunately, it's a very popular make and model; you see them everywhere. Black with heavy aluminum edging, made by Samsonite. The only distinguishing feature is a green hotel sticker I keep on one corner for purposes of identification in cloakrooms and places like that. It would not be too hard to remove."

"Which hotel, sir?"

"The Rincome. It's in Chiangmai, Thailand."

"Not too usual a sticker, then."

"That was the idea."

The inspector made a further note. When he had finished he leaned forward to suggest confidential communication. "Now, Mr. Nesbitt, I have one more question. Is it not possible that the case itself might be of more interest than you have suggested?"

Nesbitt took a deep breath to steady himself while he

did his best to keep his face impassive. "I don't understand your suggestion. I have already told you that the case is a very ordinary one and we reported the theft less than an hour ago."

Franzini put his finger tips together. "You are a very observant man; I have already noted that several times. Now consider this: you left your hotel to see some of the sights of Venice with what I understand is a most attractive lady. You had no business appointment, because you told me that you know no one here. At this excellent hotel your case would have been entirely safe in the keeping of the concierge. Yet you chose to carry it while you were escorting Miss Van Damm. How do you explain that?"

"As I told you, it contained all of my traveler's checks."

The inspector lifted his shoulders and let them fall. "The hotel safe was available and traveler's checks are easily replaced."

Nesbitt took his time. He was almost certain that somehow Franzini knew about the case — the coincidence was too marked — but at all costs he had to keep his own mouth shut. Mark Day never revealed anything, and he was the best in the business.

"I'm very used to carrying it," he began. "I've had my case for some time, it's become part of my professional life. Therefore you could say that it has for me a certain sentimental value."

"Ah!" Franzini said.

The inspector got to his feet. "I can no longer deny myself the privilege of meeting the enchanting Miss Van Damm; I have read of her so much. But first may I use your telephone? The call will not appear on your bill."

"Please."

Franzini gave a number and was connected promptly. He carried on a conversation in Italian for a minute or two and concluded by giving some instructions. After he had hung up, he turned to Nesbitt. "You will be hearing from us shortly, I hope. I shall see to this matter personally."

"I'm most grateful," Ed told him.

"Thank you. I shall also explain to the manager, who is a friend of mine, about the temporary loss of your funds. There will be no embarrassment."

"That's most considerate. And Miss Van Damm, I believe, will be up to your expectations. She's right next door."

"I know, but I shall still step out into the corridor and knock at her suite. Appearances, you understand. Thank you for your assistance."

As soon as the door was shut Ed took stock and decided that he had done all that he could for the moment. It was already too late to apply for replacement checks at Cook's and without his attaché case he could not get any work done. Rather than waste time completely, he went through his daily program of Royal Canadian Air Force exercises.

Two hours later the magic of Venice and the facilities of the Bauer Gruenwald had done much to restore sanity. He had been notified that his signature on any bills was all that would be required and that he could settle them at any time in the future. When he had called Celestine, she had accepted his dinner invitation with evident pleasure. Five minutes after the time he had set she tapped lightly on his door. He opened it to discover her more lovely than he had imagined possible. Even in the books he had written she had never been that utterly charming. *Celestine Van Damm!* It was incredible.

They went down to dinner, a handsome couple. What Nesbitt knew he lacked in himself was more than compensated for by the exquisite lady who had accepted him as her escort. Even in Venice she drew rapt attention as they entered the dining room and were seated; the service that they received immediately was a testimony to her radiant appeal. If it were not for the damning loss of his attaché case, Ed Nesbitt would have been at his zenith.

The dinner itself was superb. Part of it was the food, but the greater part was Celestine, so magically come to life, so much more of a fulfillment than he would have dared to dream. Using the imagination with which he was gifted, he allowed himself to play the role of a man suitable to be in her company, and only one person fitted that description. In his mind he added the necessary inches to his stature, erased a few years, and remolded his features and body into the image of the man he had made famous literally throughout the world.

By the time that the dessert was being served he had conquered himself. In the morning he would purchase a new case, rewrite his notes to the best of his ability, arrange to have a new copy of his itinerary sent to him, and apply for his replacement checks. He would be able to recover eighty percent of the contents of his case. As far as the case itself was concerned, he had not asked to become a dummy courier and the switch at Frankfurt had been intended to pass undetected. Perhaps the thief of the afternoon had done more damage to the people who had imposed on him than to himself. That was a comforting thought and he savored it.

"Good evening."

He looked up quickly, recognizing the voice. Inspector

Franzini had changed into a dark suit for evening, and with such telling effect that he could have stepped onto the set as the leading man in any of the potent romantic Italian movies. Had Day himself been there, they would have constituted an unbeatable pair.

"Please sit down," Nesbitt invited after he had risen, and indicated a chair.

Franzini complied. "I accept," he said, "because no true Italian could deny himself the pleasure of being seen with Miss Van Damm."

He was rewarded with a smile that should have made his knees weak, and very possibly did. "Have you eaten?" Nesbitt asked him before things got too far out of hand.

"Yes, thank you, I have."

"Then coffee perhaps?"

"If you wish, certainly." He signaled the waiter and spoke a word or two. Almost immediately a cup was produced and filled; Nesbitt noted that the inspector rated the utmost attention. Sugar and cream were tendered and used, then Franzini stirred his coffee as he spoke. "When you have finished with your dinner, Mr. Nesbitt, you can pick up your attaché case in the lobby — the concierge has it. I took the liberty of checking the contents and based on the information you gave me, they appear to be intact."

A dozen different ideas hit Ed all at the same time. To have recovered the case so quickly with nothing missing was incredible; there had to be something behind it! As that thought was uppermost he also experienced a flooding sense of relief; he had recovered everything *including* the case itself — providing it was the same one. The thieves had obviously been foiled. The Italian police had scored a remarkable victory, and Franzini was one of those Italians too handsome to be real. Fervently he hoped that he would not have to give up the most fascinating woman he had ever met in exchange for the return of his property.

He realized that he was expected to say something, in fact he was already late at the post. "That's wonderful," he exclaimed and made it sound totally sincere. "I'm amazed at your efficiency. How in the world did you recover it so quickly?"

Franzini smiled at Celestine and had some of his coffee before he replied. "We have our small ways. I am personally most happy that this time we were successful."

"I shall hate to leave your city," Nesbitt said.

"Thank you." The inspector became more serious. "If you will allow me, I venture to give you a small suggestion."

"By all means."

"Don't go to Beirut. I can well understand your professional interest in the city, and it is certainly well worth a visit on its own merits, but this is not the time."

"Because of the guerrilla activity?"

"In large part, yes. I know you for a man of unquestioned courage — that has been recently demonstrated — but there are also some other considerations of which you may not be fully aware. Because of them a prominent American, such as yourself, could be in a hazardous position. Feelings are running very high at the moment and you could be caught in a maelstrom."

Nesbitt thought. It seemed very clear to him that he was being told something, and furthermore he was expected to listen and listen carefully. But if he bypassed Beirut, not only would he miss the city famed as the spy capital of the Near East, all of his flight schedule and other reservations would be thrown out of gear.

He stalled for time. "I would have to change quite a few things on very short notice."

Franzini accepted that with a nod. "Quite true, but fortunately there is an available flight that will take you more or less directly to Istanbul. I suspect that your time will be well invested there."

That was a clue if he had ever heard one.

Celestine rose. "If you gentlemen will excuse me . . ." she said. She picked up her evening purse and left the table.

As soon as she was out of hearing range Franzini put a question. "I assume that Miss Van Damm is traveling with you. Does this complicate matters?"

"No, because we aren't traveling together. You can believe this or not as you choose, but I was surprised when I encountered her here."

The inspector considered that. "I made a misassumption; it was very careless of me. Quite possibly you did not wish your itinerary discussed so openly."

"I don't believe that it really matters." Nesbitt thought for a moment. "If I do follow your suggestion and go straight through to Istanbul, I'll have to see a travel agent and make arrangements."

"Perhaps the hotel can help. They have a good travel agent close by."

Nesbitt made a decision. "All right, I'll bypass Beirut, although I was really looking forward to going there. Incidently, you seem to have all of the details concerning my plans. Is there anything now that you would care to tell me?"

Franzini smiled. "Let it be sufficient that you have your case back." He got to his feet. "My compliments to Miss Van Damm; you are a most fortunate man. I hope that we may meet again — under agreeable circumstances."

Ed stood up too. "I'd like that, I want to come back to Venice. By the way, if you happen to see him, give my regards to Mr. Smith."

"If I encounter anyone of that name who appears to know you, I will be happy to do so. Good-night, Mr. Nesbitt."

When Celestine came back he took her out onto the dance floor. He danced moderately well, but Celestine was like a cloud in his arms. She seemed to float before him and in response he let his arm tighten about her waist.

Very quietly she whispered into his ear. "You've had a trying time. I think it would be nice if you took a lady to bed with you tonight."

That hit him; for an instant he almost froze. Then he remembered how Mark Day would handle matters and he recovered the step he had nearly missed. Without allowing himself to think of anything but the mere words, he whispered back, "Are you the lady?"

"Possibly."

The single word was intoxicating, he did not dare to contemplate what it really meant. He said nothing in reply because there were no appropriate words. When they had returned to their table he forced himself to ask if she would like anything else. When she shook her head and then gave him a fractional smile, he felt that the pulsing of

101

his blood must be visible at his temples. His body felt unnaturally warm, and impatience gnawed at him savagely. He forced himself not to betray his emotions — to take his time. He added the tip to the check when it was presented and signed it, remembering that now he would be able to settle it promptly when he checked out.

Doing his best to reveal nothing of his private thoughts he escorted Celestine out of the dining room, but it seemed that every step he took was a betrayal of his inner emotions. Together they started for the elevator, then Ed remembered. He excused himself long enough to reclaim his case from the concierge and then joined Celestine once more. They rode up together in silence, then walked down the corridor to their respective rooms. He waited while she unlocked her door and went in, but he did not say goodnight.

He still could not believe the thing that was happening to him. Once in his own room he turned on the lamps and noted that the large bed had already been turned down. He forced himself to take a few seconds to check the case — the contents seemed to be exactly as he had left them. He verified the few identifying marks he had made and determined that it was the substitute one that he had, not his original property. He would probably never see his own real case again — not that it mattered.

Because he sometimes liked to work late when he was traveling, he had a robe with him. He got out of his clothes and put it on; then he looked in the mirror, asking for reassurance. The mirror reported the facts and nothing more; the little flaws were all still there, the evidences that the smoothness of youth was forever gone. But he was still very much a man, not as young as he had once been, but considerably more knowledgeable, more successful, and he had a few dollars in the bank. He did not overrate himself; he had lost his early years, but he knew that he had received something in return. For a moment he contemplated a quick shave — his chin was a bit rough — then he discarded the notion.

There was a small noise at the connecting door. His heart pounding in spite of himself, he walked across the room at his normal pace and opened it. He had to pull hard a second time, but it yielded without too much noise.

Celestine stood there. She seemed a little smaller without her heels, but her hair, which she had let down, seized his attention. It fell like a miniature cascade over the pale yellow silk robe she wore, which was made more subtle with a subdued pattern of woven bamboo leaves. He looked at her face and then stepped back to invite her in. She came, stopped, and smiled at him.

He was not a lover, he knew that. He had written too many scenes that had been agonizing for him because he knew that he lacked the magic touch, the technique of the man who truly knows how. He could not pretend now, he could only be himself. He took her into his arms and felt the surge of vitality that came with her close proximity. She lifted her head a little and slightly parted her lips. He reached down only a little way to kiss her, and his blood boiled through his veins.

When he had done that he released her, walked over to the bed, and turned off one of the two lamps that lit the room. He did not trust himself to speak because he felt that his voice would betray him. He was on Olympus and, like brave Odysseus, his knees were feeble.

With the exquisite sensibility that he knew she possessed, Celestine walked to the other side of the bed. She paused for a moment and smiled, giving him the confidence that he needed to forget forever his own limitations. Then, very casually, she laid her robe aside and slipped into the bed.

Gad, she was beautiful!

He had seen her body for only a moment, but it was like ecstasy. Because he knew himself to be ten pounds too heavy, he turned his back as he laid his own robe aside. Just as he did so, the other light went out.

He got into bed and the fire seized him. Her warmth, her softness, and her unbelievable desirability overwhelmed him. She came very close and their bodies were side by side. A fragment of thought about Tristan and Isolde tried to gain recognition and failed. In his arms he held all of the wonders of paradise and the climax of his existence was at hand.

As the city of Istanbul lay spread out below him, for a few moments he felt that the Arabian Nights too had come into dramatic being. He saw the Bosporus and the Sea of Marmara whose very name was poetry as he spoke it silently to himself. A moment later he identified the Golden Horn as the aircraft sank lower. A thought hit him and on impulse he offered a mental prayer — thanking his Creator for the opportunity to see with his own eyes these far and exotic places of the world.

The travel service in Venice had been notably efficient. Signor Riccardo Guetta had assumed the details personally and before his expertise difficulties evaporated. Cancellations were accomplished and new reservations set up in a minimum of time. Nesbitt admired it all and gladly put his name into a book that the agency manager — praise be — already had in his library. It was all accomplished so smoothly that it never occurred to Ed Nesbitt that since he had supplied a copy of his itinerary to Morgan in Vienna, the changes which were being made might cause some confusion.

As he came out of the customs area at the airport he was met by another of the experienced transfer men who seemed to possess second sight when it came to identifying their clients in the midst of a small mass of other travelers. This one was thin, dark, and hawk-nosed, but his manner was cordial and businesslike. "There were some small problems concerning reservations," he informed Nesbitt. "However, they are all straightened out now. We have you in the Divan, which is a very good hotel."

"That will be fine," Ed said. "What do you have on the schedule?"

"I would recommend lunch at the hotel, sir, the dining room is quite good. This afternoon, if you wish, I will be your guide to see St. Sophie's, the Blue Mosque, and, if we have time, the Topkapi Palace."

"That sounds very interesting, but I particularly want to experience the ordinary life of the city; I'm less interested in the tourist attractions."

"To what extent, sir?"

Ed answered that one quickly. "Don't misunderstand me — I'm not looking for any lady friends or anything like that. I'm an author who likes to write about cities in countries other than my own."

The transfer man lit up. "It will be a great pleasure, then, to show you some of the real life in our city. I, too, hope to be a writer someday. I have been educated with this in view. I am honored to be your guide. Let me get the baggage."

In ten minutes they were in a taxi bound for the city proper. "Your hotel is on the European side, north of the Golden Horn; it is a very good location," the guide declared. "I must tell you my name. In Turkish you could not, I believe, pronounce it, so I have chosen an American name for my English-speaking guests. It is Peter. I also speak French; when I have French tourists they call me Pierre."

"A good arrangement; Peter it is. My name is Nesbitt."

"That I understand, sir. I also understand that you have," he lowered his voice so that the taxi driver could not hear, ". . . a very important mission."

Ed looked at him. "I don't follow you."

"Of course, I understand. You may trust me. Someday I too would like to work for the American CIA. I shall do my best for you and after that, perhaps you will recommend me. I am intelligent and I know very much how to keep my mouth shut."

"That is a most valuable gift. Remember that I am an author and that is all — do I make myself clear?"

"Perfectly. It is, what you call, an excellent cover. No one will ever suspect. Even here in Turkey we know the name of Mr. Mark Day. No one will know that now we entertain him in person. How is the wonderful Miss Van Damm?"

That brought up a recent memory too precious to be shared with anyone. After a moment or two he replied. "When I saw her in Venice just before I came here, she was fine."

The guide sighed. "I do wish that you had chosen to bring her to Turkey. Then I could at least have a look."

"Possibly you may," Nesbitt said.

He liked the Divan immediately; it was clean and inviting and the air suggested good service and accommodations. He signed the register, made an appointment with Peter for guide service immediately after lunch, and then followed the bellboy up to his room. After he was installed, he spent five minutes at the window drinking in Istanbul, then he prepared for lunch.

The dining room was located on the second floor, with a wide and inviting staircase leading up from the lobby. Before he went in to eat, Nesbitt stopped for a moment to study the layout, visualizing what action might take place there in some future book. From his vantage point he saw a couple leaving the hotel. They came to his notice because they seemed to be hurrying: walking just a little too fast. If they had been coming in he would not have paid them any particular attention — they could be returning from a tour and anxious to find the washroom — but there was a certain anxiety in their manner that he could read even as he looked down at a fairly steep angle.

Then he froze, holding himself perfectly still so that he would not betray his own presence by any quick motion that might attract attention. He was successful; neither of the two people he was watching thought to look upward as they headed as quickly as they reasonably could toward the exit and a taxi that was already waiting with its door open. He could not be absolutely certain of the man's identity because he did not get a clear look at his face, but he was almost positive that it was the George Smith he had met in Morgan's office in Vienna, the man who was "with the government."

It could well be, he had gathered that Smith moved about quite a bit. It was even possible that he was in Istanbul because he wanted to keep his dummy courier under surveillance; he had more or less promised to do that. That made things much more interesting from Nesbitt's point of view; perhaps he was on a more important mission than he knew.

It was the woman who threw him, because he knew her positively — even the way she walked. She was the supposed reporter he had met at Frankfurt, the one who had called herself Gretel Hoffmeister.

7

WHILE HE ATE his lunch, Ed Nesbitt did some very hard thinking. Too much was going on that he did not understand and he was determined to correct that situation one way or another. Meanwhile uncertainty, frustration, and plain anger were building up within him. He knew that he would have to keep these emotions under control, but he didn't expect it was going to be easy. The very realization of his position made him angrier still.

Consciously he went back to the beginning and began to assemble the known facts in his mind.

He had been duped in Frankfurt — there was no doubt about that. The substitution of attaché cases was definite; the probabilities were that he was not supposed to have detected it.

Therefore his call at the American Embassy in Vienna had not been anticipated. However, when he got there they had known who he was and had taken some action — after he had been interviewed by Windress and had more or less forced his way in to see Morgan.

Morgan had to be genuine — a fake setup within the walls of the embassy was almost impossible to imagine. To make doubly sure, he could check with the USIA and he resolved to do that.

Accepting Morgan for the moment as genuine, then his introduction of George Smith as "with the government" had to be taken at its face value. Furthermore, Smith was clearly in a position of some authority. The most obvious thought was the CIA, but there were hundreds of other divisions and branches of the government — some well-known and some, presumably, not known at all.

Nesbitt was almost certain that it was Smith he had seen within the hour. Assuming that he was in some sort of intelligence work, then his turning up in Istanbul was not too unusual. He had promised that he was going to keep watch over Nesbitt, but that certainly didn't imply that he intended to do it personally.

So far, so good.

But it was definitely Gretel Hoffmeister he had spotted in the lobby. And, if his other identification had been correct, she had been in the company of George Smith.

Was Gretel, therefore also "with the government?" If she was, then why, in the name of heaven, had she been pointed toward him? That brought up another question: while Morgan had been going through the motions of checking up on her in Nesbitt's presence, had he already known that she was a government agent — presuming that she was?

He ordered dessert and then considered another piece of evidence: the obvious haste on the part of Gretel and (probably) George Smith to get out of the hotel. A very likely explanation for that presented itself: they had just learned that their pet pigeon had arrived a day early and they wanted to be out of his sight ASAP. The more he considered that idea, the more he believed it. He definitely was not supposed to see them and most of all not together. But he had and, fortunately, they did not know it as yet. That gave him a good card he could play when the proper time came.

There remained one more conclusion and it did not escape him: if Gretel — or whatever her real name was — was a colleague of Smith's, then whatever was concealed in the attaché case he carried had been planted there not by some unseen foreign power, but by the United States Government itself.

His meditations were interrupted by the arrival of Peter who presented himself as eager to begin the afternoon program of sightseeing. At Nesbitt's invitation he sat down and almost at once became confidential. "Mr. Nesbitt, sir, will you allow me a suggestion?"

"Go ahead."

"You are here presumably as a tourist, as so many others have come in the past. Therefore it will be thought very strange if you do not start out by visiting some of the most famous attractions. This need not take much of your time, but if you are, perhaps, being observed, it would strengthen your cover if you do what is expected of you. Otherwise . . ." He shrugged his shoulders.

Nesbitt decided to play the game. "Where must we go?" he asked.

Peter leaned forward and restrained his long fingers from tracing patterns on the tablecloth. "The Blue Mosque, certainly, with its six minarets; you wouldn't want to miss it in any event. St. Sophie's, which everyone should see, the cisterns, Topkapi Palace, and the Grand Bazaar. All are most interesting. At Topkapi you can see the actual jeweled dagger about which the famous movie was made, and also the real hand of John the Baptist."

"It sounds like quite an afternoon."

"Indeed, sir, it is actually more than an afternoon, but we can make detours as you see fit."

Nesbitt finished his coffee and signed the check. "I'm ready," he announced. "Let's do two or three things and then get to the Grand Bazaar about four or so. It will still be open, won't it?"

"Oh, certainly. It is a fantastic place. It will be very exciting for me to accompany you today."

They set out from the hotel with the usual arrangement: a car and driver that constituted an inseparable combination, with themselves as client and guide. As they drove Peter recited all of the usual facts about the city once known as Constantinople, which had reigned during one period in history as the largest metropolis in the world. To the standard discourse he added a few variations in honor of Nesbitt, pointing out from time to time the sites of particularly infamous crimes or other events connected with violence.

With understandable pride Peter displayed a tall Egyptian obelisk that retained its atmosphere of mystery even after ages and then lectured on the great beauty of the

Blue Mosque. It was indeed an architectural jewel that deserved its vast reputation.

The cisterns brought antiquity almost within reach, as Nesbitt studied their construction and tried to imagine the incredible amount of human labor that had gone into their construction. He lingered longer than was necessary to fix clearly in his mind their underground vastness, the placement of the pillars, and the possibility that they might serve as the setting for some highly suspenseful action. But even as he took in the scene that contained so many elements of the macabre, the eerie, and the suggestion of a vast entrance into some unknown world, he could not escape the feeling that he had seen it somewhere before.

Then he remembered. *"From Russia With Love?"* he asked.

Peter nodded and thereby erased his hopes. "Yes, Mr. James Bond was here; not everyone remembers." It had been a good idea while it had lasted, but it was gone now; someone else had found it first.

When they were back in the car, Peter was ready to show him more. "We will go now to the Grand Bazaar," he said. "It is something I think you will like very much. It is all under cover and it is very large. There are not many things you cannot buy there; there are four thousand shops. But the wandering sellers, what is the word . . . ?"

"Peddlers?"

"Yes, peddlers, they are not reliable."

"For the average tourist the bazaar is a safe place to visit?"

"But of course! So many merchants depend on it for their living, they cannot allow it to become dangerous."

"That makes sense," Ed agreed. He remained silent, still

remembering the cisterns, until the car was threading its way the last few feet in toward one of the entrances to the bazaar. Then he awoke. The atmosphere was wonderful: there were people in native Turkish dress flowing back and forth, de luxe shops that had been set up just outside of the bazaar itself to attract the carriage trade, and everywhere the sounds of a great market — the babble of voices, the shuffling of feet, and a constant undertone that was like the unceasing sound of the sea in a freshening wind.

Nesbitt turned to his guide. "This is just what I hoped it would be," he said. "Since it is perfectly safe, I'd like to explore on my own — do you mind?"

"You will get lost," Peter warned, "and people here do not always speak English."

"Still, I want to try."

"If you wish, then go. I will wait here for you. Do you think you can keep your bearings?"

"I believe so."

"Then good luck, and remember never to pay the first price for anything."

"I don't plan to do any buying; I just want to see the bazaar my own way."

Peter hesitated. "Would you like to leave your case with me?" he asked.

Nesbitt shook his head. "I always carry it," he replied. "I might change my mind about buying something and I like to take notes."

He was not sure whether Peter had betrayed the slightest indication of disappointment, but it did not really matter. Even though he was paying for guide service, he wanted the mild adventure of seeing the Grand Bazaar on his own and if he got lost, then he would have to find his own way out. He was confident that he could do it. He knew that his sense of direction was unusually good. And even in a Turkish bazaar, there would be some who would be able to understand his language.

From the moment that he walked inside he was glad of his decision: the place was fascinating. The shops seemed without number, but they were aligned in neat rows like a complete city under a roof. He went past displays of hardware and household goods, of glass and china, of candles and electrical supplies. He turned down another miniature street and found that he was in a maze of fabrics and goods of every kind made of cloth. The selection offered seemed limitless; clearly modern Turkey had everything available that any reasonable person could want.

He wandered farther and found himself in an area where alabaster and onyx in the form of vases, dishes, and accessories were on display. All of the stores seemed to be crammed with merchandise; inventory apparently was no problem here. He was tempted many times to buy, and only the question of safe shipment home deterred him. He also learned that in the shops which sold goods that might appeal to tourists, English was almost always spoken. He had been in the bazaar more than three quarters of an hour, having one of the best times of his life, before he finally detected that he was being followed.

At first it did not bother him at all. He had not been able to glimpse whoever it was that was tagging his progress, but the most likely explanation was Peter who, understandably enough, was doing his duty by keeping a precautionary watch over his client. There was the possibility that it was one of George Smith's people; it was made somewhat more likely by the glimpse he was almost sure he had had of Smith himself in the hotel lobby.

Another possibility was that it was simply a curiosity seeker who had taken it upon himself to observe what the foreigner was doing. He wondered if it would be worthwhile to try and slip the tag. Mark Day did that easily enough at almost any time, but now there were no busses to be caught at the last moment, no hotels with multiple entrances, or any courtyards to slip through with high board fences in urgent need of repair. In the bazaar, which after all was laid out very much on the grid system, it was another matter entirely. None of the shops appeared to have any rear exits he could use, and there were no unknown persons to whisper, "*Quick, sir, follow me!*"

Picking a passageway at random, but still carefully noting its direction, Nesbitt started out walking at his fastest pace. He gave every appearance of a man in a hurry, someone who had spent too long in the bazaar and who was striving to catch up with the tourist group of which he was a part. He attracted very little attention, but the swiftness of his pace would automatically make it much more difficult for his shadow to keep up without showing himself very plainly in the open.

As he strode briskly down the avenue he had selected, he still took in the various displays, at least in part. The utilitarian section was behind him; he was coming into a sector devoted to the arts and crafts. He saw many wonderful things even at his rapid pace and he had a desire to look at them more closely.

There was no real reason why he should not do so.

To his right he saw an arts and crafts store that appeared to be unusually large for the area. It had an attractive window display and gave every external evidence of being a long-established and responsible business. Just as he came opposite the door Nesbitt stopped, faced in the direction from which he had just come, and pretended to look at a camel saddle on view in the side window.

After twenty seconds there was no sign of his tag and he thought it quite possible that he had scared the man off. Then he realized that he was in a highly visible position; literally a standing target in case anyone was interested. He didn't consider that too strong a possibility, but still he turned and entered the store.

He was surprised to see how high it was. The main sales floor was well-filled with merchandise, and above it there were at least two balconies that held and displayed a variety of additional items. As he walked toward the rear, a clerk came to meet him. Before the man could speak Nesbitt asked, "May I go upstairs?" At the same time he gestured and lifted his eyebrows in case he had not been understood.

The clerk spoke English. "Please," he responded, and gestured to where an open stairway at the rear led upwards. Nesbitt climbed at a steady pace, conscious only of the fact that he was reducing his visibility with every step that he took. As soon as he reached the first balcony he saw open steps which led still higher; without hesitation he took them. As he climbed he noted that the first balcony had a series of short aisles, so presumably the upper balcony would offer an equal chance to make himself temporarily invisible. And if he placed himself properly, he might also be able to look down and see who, if anyone, was coming into the shop behind him.

He waited for two long minutes, but nothing whatever

117

happened. It was then that he began to wonder if he had
been fleeing from a phantom; he had never actually seen
anyone behind him, he had just had a feeling that he was
not alone. That kind of evidence was not very substantial;
furthermore every ten seconds that passed with no one
showing up who seemed to be interested in him increased
the likelihood that he was suffering from a mild case of
nerves.

Since he had accepted the hospitality of the shop, he
knew that he would have to show some interest in the many
obviously fine things that were on display; in response he
set his case down in a safe place and began to look at some
of the offerings. They were better than he had realized, in
particular there was a series of silver-and-copper round
trays that were mounted on light legs for use as tabletops.
They were intricately worked in some fascinating patterns
that showed ancient warriors riding to battle in their
chariots and other scenes which seemed to have been taken
from the Arabian Nights.

Despite himself Nesbitt was fascinated. He had not intended to do any shopping in the bazaar, but these were
very different and would certainly fit well into his home if
he could find a satisfactory way to ship them back. He gave
his attention to six or seven of the trays and then selected
one that was about eighteen inches in diameter. He had no
idea what the price would be, but he was certainly interested enough to ask. With the tray in his hands he turned —
and froze. There was a man on the balcony behind him
leaning on the railing. Across the court there was another
on the opposite side who was watching him intently. And,
he saw in the same stricken glance, there was a third just
coming silently up the last few steps from below.

118

They could have been store personnel or customers, but he knew instantly that they were something else entirely. He saw the same flatness of expression he had described so often in print in each face, the same look of the professional, and he knew that he was the target. If he had any doubt, the man already on the balcony held his attaché case in his hand.

In that stricken moment an absurd sequence flashed through Nesbitt's mind: a scene he had written just before he had started on his trip. Mark Day and Celestine were sitting together on the Riviera talking between themselves. "I know," Day had said, "that one day they will catch up with me — I can't go on forever. No one can. But when things run out on me and I have to face the opposition for the last time, however many of them there are, I'm going to do my best to make them pay. Whoever is the most important, the most valuable man to their side, is the one I'll go for first. After that I'll take as many as I can until . . ." He had left the sentence unfinished.

In the paralyzing silence Ed Nesbitt knew that he faced that same situation. They would not be content merely to take his case; they were there to settle with him, finally and permanently.

He was not about to give up without an effort to bluff his way out. He made an instant decision to forego the case — it was the only thing he could do. Holding the tray just as though he had selected it to purchase, he started toward the steps. He had taken two paces when he looked into the face of the man who was waiting for him there and knew that it was hopeless. They would be armed, of course, and silencers would be screwed on the ends of the barrels of their guns. But until one of them made an overt act, he was going to continue to try.

Then he remembered. As he had for so long trained it to do, his mind blotted out his own limitations and shifted almost instantly into the alter ego with which it was so familiar.

Mark Day knew that the situation was desperate; he was unarmed and there was no possible way of reaching the man who was at least twenty feet away on the other side of the balcony. The open court was between them and he was himself pitilessly exposed. Since he had started for the stairway, he kept on until he was directly at the top step looking down at the man who was waiting for him just below, blocking his way.

"Excuse me," Day said, and started down.

Without warning the man sprang and seized him by the left ankle. That was an overt act, a license for Mark to protect himself. He threw his entire weight onto his left leg and simultaneously bent his knee, making it momentarily impossible for the man to yank his leg forward. That gave him three fifths of a second which was enough; his right foot was already off the floor and partially cocked behind him. With the skill he had developed during hundreds of hours of practice in the karate dojo he snapped his body to the left and as he did so executed the difficult but enormously effective roundhouse kick. The power of his leg muscles was augmented mightily by the sudden movement of his pelvis; as a result his leg moved with the speed of a whip. The toe of his shoe hit directly behind the left ear of the man who held his ankle. The shock of the impact told him that he had been fearfully successful; the hand on his ankle went limp.

He wasted no precious time watching the man fall; he was done for and not a split second more could be devoted to him. Whirling his body fully around Mark saw that the man fourteen feet from him on the balcony had a gun in his hand; he was only waiting for Day to stop moving for an instant so that he could shoot with fatal accuracy.

At that desperate moment Mark considered the heavy metal tray he still held as a possible shield. It would not do, it was much too small; whatever part of his body he might attempt to protect, the rest would be left wide open to attack. The force of the kick he had just delivered had compelled him to hold the tray close to his body on the left hand side; his hands still grasping it by the rim. With that instinct that comes to trapped animals and desperate men, Day wasted not a precious instant; he used the force of his shoulders and right upper arm to fling the tray like a discus directly at the man with the gun.

Mark fully expected to feel the impact of a bullet entering his body, but the sudden, violent need for self-protection had caused the gunman to try to jerk himself backward out of the way. The heavy tray struck him with its spinning serrated edge on the side of his neck with an awful impact. His chin snapped up and his knees unlocked. As Day hit the floor like a good infantryman caught in the open, the man uttered one very quick sound that had nothing in it that was human; it was a truncated scream of utter anguish that comes just before extinction. The man jerked his arm forward in an animal attempt to regain his balance; as he did so the gun fell from his fingers. His body arced backwards across the railing, hung there all but motionless for the greater part of two seconds, and then tipped over. Head downward, he plunged toward the main floor twenty-five feet below.

It wasn't over yet; very clearly Mark saw the man on the opposite side of the balcony and the gun that he held in his two hands, poised to fire. He couldn't do so while the body of his partner was still between them, but it would all be over in a scant second or two.

Instinct and long training told Day what to do. Jamming the palm of his left hand against the floor, and using what purchase he could get with his feet, he rammed his body forward until the fingers of his right hand reached the gun that the falling man had dropped. Then he whipped his body over until he had a partial cover behind a small roll of hand-crafted rugs that lay on the floor.

He did not hear the sound of the shot, but he knew that a bullet had buried itself in the rugs very close to his head. Taking advantage of the momentary bit of security provided by the merciful rugs, he sighted his opponent over the top of the barrel of the gun he held and pulled the trigger.

Ed Nesbitt had never before fired a gun in his life. He knew very little about them apart from what his profession had required him to learn. From where he lay on the floor he watched the man he had just shot across the opening that was less than ten yards wide. It never occurred to him to fire again; he somehow sensed that there was no need.

The man stood there, his gun lowered, the only expression on his face one of vacant surprise. Even at the distance Ed could see his eyes lose their focus, then his knees folded and he went down without a sound except for the mechanical noises of his body as it crumpled to the floor.

Nesbitt stood up. For several seconds he did not know what else to do, then he bent over and picked up the tray he had thrown. Its sharply worked edge was stained with blood, but that would wash off. He picked up his attaché case in his left hand and with the plate in his right he walked down the stairs, stepping carefully over the inert man who had attempted to block his way. He knew that there were people present, those who worked in the store, but he had other things on his mind.

He gained the main floor and since no one intercepted him, he went forward to the desk beside the front door. There was a man behind it, watching him as though he had been fascinated by some lethal cobra about to strike. Since the store employee seemed too transfixed to say anything, Nesbitt put down the tray he was carrying on the counter top and spoke in a normal tone of voice. "If this tabletop isn't too much," he said, "I'd like to buy it, along with a set of legs, of course."

8

By the time that the hour of midnight hung in the rich Turkish sky above Istanbul, the quantity of communications that had been built up concerning the incident in the Grand Bazaar was approaching the fantastic. On Ataturk Boulevard in Ankara the lights had been kept burning for some time at the American Embassy. A number of messages had come in from the Central Intelligence Agency, from the FBI, from various branches of the State Department, and from Interpol. The traffic was equally heavy at the Istanbul police headquarters and when the birth of the new day occurred, the volume had not slackened. Ed Nesbitt himself was not personally concerned; at the hotel's suggestion he had booked a night tour of the city and was absorbing with interest the muscular skills of one of the city's more appealing belly dancers.

He had, of course, been interviewed and he had answered a number of questions. Then, after having dinner, he had gone out on the tour partly for enjoyment and also to be a little less available for at least a few hours. If they really wanted him, they would have no trouble picking him up. When the nubile young woman with the remarkably fluent hips chose him as the subject of her special attentions as she danced, he was captivated to the point where he had very nearly put the whole thing out of his mind. Definitely Mark Day would have to encounter this exotic creature except that she would probably dance for him alone, in the moonlight of the hours before dawn, in some private place where her lithe body could be free of all restraining garments. A woman like that was born to dance nude, to crown her art with the perfection of her body undisfigured by any kind of costume. For Ed Nesbitt that was out of the question, but Mark Day would be able to arrange it — he always succeeded where women were concerned and left them grateful that he had. He watched the dancer carefully and engraved her image on his memory.

As she raised her arms and swayed for yet another time, two men were in conference together in a very private room where they had met before. One of them was an American, the other Turkish; they were very close friends as well as being, to a certain degree, colleagues. Since the Turkish officer spoke effortless English, they conversed in that language. Between them there was a small table, elaborately inlaid, that held a pot of thick Turkish coffee along with some sweetmeats.

"I got here as soon as I could, Ahmet," the American said. "You can understand that I have been busy."

"Of course, and so have we. There are now many things I would like to ask you." He poured coffee and offered a small cup to his guest. "It is understood," he added, "that whatever is said in this room tonight remains forever just between us. You have my word that we are not being overheard — I can absolutely guarantee it."

The American drank a little of the coffee and then set the cup carefully down. "I will do the very best that I can," he promised.

"I understand. Now, since my lips are forever sealed, will you please tell me who this Edwin Nesbitt is?"

"He's an American author of espionage novels; a very successful and popular one. He writes under his own name and the basic facts about him are all in *Who's Who*."

"I have already read them."

"Good. One point: he is a bear on getting all of his backgrounds and other details right; he does a great deal of research. That's generally agreed to be one of the reasons for his wide readership. Also he treats his hero quite realistically; you can actually believe in him, unless, of course, you know too much about the business."

The Turkish officer shrugged. "We do not exactly live in a vacuum here, we all know about Mark Day. I now return to my original question: granting that his cover is superb, who is Nesbitt?"

"Ahmet, that's it! If you don't believe me I can't truly blame you, but he definitely isn't on our staff, for instance. I'll give you a little more — to the best of my knowledge, and you have my word on that, he isn't with Naval Intelligence or any of the other similar organizations; at least they all swear that he isn't."

Ahmet refilled his coffee cup and eased back in his chair. "I am forced to believe you because I always have. One more question: is it possible that he belongs to some bureau, like Quiller's, that officially doesn't exist?"

The American shook his head. "To the very best of my knowledge, no."

His colleague leaned forward and focused his attention. "Very well, how then do you explain what happened this afternoon? *Three armed men* ambushed him when he was alone and had no weapon whatever that we know of. Furthermore, they were not amateurs. He took all three before they really knew what hit them." He tapped his forefinger on the American's knee. "George, you know as well as I do that only a superb professional could do that!"

His friend looked at him. "It's unlikely as all hell, but that's what happened. How many witnesses did you dig up?"

"Six, and they all agree. But, my friend, *that isn't all.* You know what happened in Berlin, of course."

"I do, and I can't explain that either."

Ahmet leaned back once more and spread his hands, palms up. "So you see, we have here in protective coloration a man of truly extraordinary ability. Obviously a karate expert; that kick he administered to the skull was delivered within half an inch of the exact spot and it was marvelously focused."

George interrupted. "That I *can* explain. Mark Day does a good deal of fighting, of course you know that. To keep it realistic Nesbitt has taken karate himself for years. I

told you that he is a crank on accuracy. I just learned tonight that he's had some lessons from Nishiyama himself."

"Black belt?"

"I don't know, but he's obviously good. He must have the
reflexes of a lynx."

"True. Also, my friend, a formidable marksman. While
out of position and being shot at he fires one round . . ."
Once more he spread his hands in the same eloquent gesture. "We have some very good men with us — some excellent men — but coolness and action like that takes tremendous training and years of experience. Please do not
try to convince me any differently."

"All right," the American said, "I won't."

"That is good, because if you did I would remind you of
his performance in Berlin. True that was only one opponent, *but do you know who it was?*"

"Please tell me."

"He has a half dozen names, but we coded him as Feodor."

For a moment the American looked genuinely stunned,
obviously he had not known that. "You mean the same
man . . .?"

"I do. According to . . . certain sources of information . . .
he had been responsible for ending the careers of at least
three very good agents of friendly powers — friendly to us,
that is. Probably there were many more, especially if you
count civilians and innocent bystanders. A sort of human
barracuda. *That* is the man your Mr. Nesbitt disposed of
so neatly!"

George Smith stood up. "All right, I've got to agree with
you despite everything I've been told. He has to be a pro,
and a helluva good one. Nothing else fits. I'll continue

checking until I get some kind of an answer. In the meantime, assume that he belongs to us, because if he doesn't then I'm really at sea."

Ahmet rose also. "I shall do that. When you do find out, my deepest compliments to whoever trained him. One more thing: he has presented us with three personages, two fortunately still living, whom we very much desire to have. I am ashamed to inform you that we were not even aware that one of them was here."

"You're entirely welcome."

"It is very good to have them out of circulation. You do not mind if we keep Mr. Nesbitt under cautious observation while he chooses to honor us with his presence? Someone should be there to tidy up behind him."

"By all means. We're doing that too — or we thought that we were."

"I'm glad you told me that; I will advise our own people. I wonder what he plans for tomorrow."

"He's scheduled to visit the Topkapi Palace."

"May Allah preserve peace and our precious relics!"

"I'm sure that He will. Good-night, Ahmet."

"Good-night, George. Sleep well."

When Peter the guide arrived at nine the following morning to pick up his charge, he was in a state of mixed emotions. He had had a brief and fitful night's sleep, after spending the greater part of the evening in grueling conversation with the authorities. He had repeated his story a dozen times and had undergone the most searching questioning he could imagine. Every chance remark that the American Nesbitt had uttered in his presence he had been expected to recall verbatim, and any lapse of memory on his part had been regarded with extreme suspicion. It had been especially difficult for him to explain how he had allowed his client to venture unaccompanied into the vast maze of the Grand Bazaar. It had not been an experience he wished to repeat.

On the other hand, never in his career had he had a client that so filled him with a sense of awe. After escorting a steady stream of camera-carrying Americans and Japanese, he suddenly found himself assisting what had to be the most formidable secret agent his mind could imagine. The fact that this man did not look the part only enhanced the great privilege that was his, because he shared the secret of his true identity. Not by chapter and verse, but enough to satisfy him completely. He looked forward to a thrilling day.

This time he most carefully remembered every word that Nesbitt spoke, almost every gesture that he made. When they reached the Topkapi Palace, Peter paid the most intricate attention also to everything that his client did, and noted precisely every display that captured his attention. Nothing happened that was in the least unusual, nothing that is, until Nesbitt turned to him just before lunch and remarked, "I wish those people would stop following us all of the time."

Peter's pulse leaped in his veins, because there was a chance he would be able to see the man he was with in action. Because he had been alerted, he too began to watch for the people who were following them. No thought of personal danger entered his mind; he was with the agent Nesbitt and that was all the assurance he required. Presently he was able to detect the presence of at least one man who seemed to be with them wherever they went, unobtrusively somewhere in the background. That was proof once again of what he already knew about his client, and a savage tingling thrill ran the length of his spine. Perhaps, when it happened, he himself might be found worthy of a small bit of the action, provided, of course, that he did not get in Nesbitt's way.

Unfortunately, there was no action at all. When the day's sightseeing had been concluded, nothing of a dramatic nature had occurred. Peter suggested a night excursion, something he usually wished to avoid, but Nesbitt seemed inclined to rest and take a leisurely dinner before planning anything further.

Peter did not give up. "*Effendi,*" he said. "I know of your interest in things that, let us say, the common tourist would never see. You have already experienced the usual night-club tour and I understand how it must have bored you."

"I am not looking for a woman," Nesbitt told him.

"Oh, I know that, sir, Miss Van Damm must be more than any man could desire."

"She is," Ed told him quite truthfully.

"There are in this city many places that are known only to us who live here. You can see performances of belly dance and other arts that you will find nowhere else. I do not speak of sex shows, to a man of your caliber they would hold no interest, but if you wish for some genuine atmosphere . . ."

Unwittingly, perhaps, he had chosen precisely the right word. Nesbitt was very interested in atmosphere. "I presume that it would be safe," he said.

Peter was amused — such a question from this man was a rich jest. "At the most, a little light exercise. Nothing more."

"What time should we leave?"

"At nine thirty, sir, I will call for you."

Thus it was decided that a number of the duty personnel of the Turkish police, as well as several other organizations, were called upon to put in overtime. Peter did indeed know the city of Istanbul very well and he took Nesbitt, plus his unseen retinue, on an extensive tour that only ended when the sun was threatening to kindle the eastern sky. Nesbitt was richly satisfied; he had had a most entertaining and productive evening that had provided him with a wealth of material he could use. All this came at astonishingly small expense; they had gone into place after place where a few whispered words between Peter and the management had somehow forestalled the presentation of the check. "The manager insists," Peter had told him time after time. "It is so seldom that a foreigner comes here, they are honored. Also they hope that you may mention the establishment someday in one of your future books."

This arrangement Nesbitt had protested, but there was no way that he could force reluctant proprietors to present a tab, especially when they were all apparently unable to understand a word of the only language he could speak. The suspicion was in his mind that Peter's introductions of him contained something more than a reference to his literary works, but he had no ear whatever for Turkish and he knew better than to ask.

When at last the two weary men, and their even wearier invisible entourage, returned to the Divan, Nesbitt was sincere in his thanks to his more than dutiful guide. Thus encouraged, Peter asked for, and received, his idol's private home address. As he gave it, Nesbitt knew what he would probably receive — a carefully worded plea for help in reaching the United States. Again perhaps not, Peter seemed happy in his work and he was already a success on his home ground. There was no reason for him to believe that Turks were anything less than content in their own country; they were free of communist domination if nothing else.

Peter saw Nesbitt off at the airport the following morning. So did six other citizens of the republic, who were infinitely grateful when the mighty jet charged down the runway, rotated, and then lifted off. They continued to watch, just to be certain that it was not coming back, until it had turned eastward and became a lost speck in the sky.

It was evening before Nesbitt reached Bombay. He had busied himself during the long flight catching up on his notes. The briefcase he had was still the substitute one that had been planted on him in Frankfurt, but so far he had not detected anything about it that betrayed its secret contents. Obviously the insertion had been a professional job; he wondered if by any chance it had been done, say, in the state of Virginia.

As he stepped off the plane, India greeted him with a blast of heat for which he was quite unprepared. It was like a furnace even though it was very late in the day. He followed the long line of passengers into the terminal and submitted himself and his luggage once more to customs inspection. He was detained somewhat longer than he had expected, apparently the official who was examining his effects was unwilling to believe that an American tourist did not carry a camera. It was explained two or three times that there was nothing illegal about bringing any kind of a camera into India, but it would have to be registered in order to insure that he took it out again when he left. Otherwise one hundred percent duty would be charged and a number of questions would have to be answered.

When at last it was all over and he was officially admitted into the country for a stay of three weeks, he was met in the lounge by an Indian who spoke English with the very tip of his tongue and lips. He pronounced his words carefully and precisely, but he still carried the suggestion of a lisp.

"Good evening. Mr. Nesbitt, sir, welcome to India. Here, let me take your case for you."

Apparently no one was willing to credit an American with being able-bodied enough to carry an attaché case. "That's all right," Nesbitt told him, "I feel naked without it."

"Just as you wish, sir. You are to stay at the Taj Mahal Hotel, it is indeed very fine and I am sure that you will enjoy your stay."

"I thought the Taj was at Agra."

"Indeed it is, sir, the name of the hotel is only taken from our most famous attraction. Please to follow me, sir, the car is waiting."

The vehicle, when he saw it, reminded Nesbitt of his early boyhood. "You must excuse the car that it is not a new one," his guide explained. "Here in India we have certain regulations we must follow. It is forbidden to bring any cars into the country. You may only buy the India-made car and for that you must wait at least two years."

"How good is the car?"

"It is terrible, sir, but they are working on improvements. You must understand that our country has many problems and we must protect our foreign exchange. The only way a foreign car can be acquired is by obtaining it from a diplomatic official when he leaves the country. When such a car becomes available, then it is allowed for one of the tourist organizations to buy it."

"But you can bring in parts, can't you?"

"Alas no, sir, that is also forbidden. So we keep them running as long as we can and it is often that we are forced to improvise. However we have some very good mechanics and they are able to make do."

As they rode in from the airport Nesbitt could see that Bombay appeared to be built on a vast arc of water that formed its harbor. After a ride of some minutes they reached a long bridge which had an ominous break in the railing a hundred-odd feet from the end.

"It was here that we have just had an unusual accident," the guide explained with a clear determination to provide a complete commentary. "A taxi was crossing the bridge with a passenger on the way to the airport when the driver suddenly beheld a ghost in the middle of the roadway. He swerved at once to avoid hitting the spirit of the deceased and unfortunately went over the edge into the water. So did his passenger, of course, who regrettably did not make his plane."

"That is a new one," Nesbitt commented.

"Not entirely, sir. Ghosts, or perhaps the same one, have been seen on many occasions at the same place and there have been other accidents as a result. We try to watch for them now."

Nesbitt thought that one over and decided that if he put

135

it into one of his books, no one would believe it. Nevertheless, the break in the bridge was material proof that something had happened. He was still turning the idea over in
his mind when the car at last drew up on the left before
the Taj Mahal Hotel. "Before we dismount, sir . . ." The
guide was at it again. "Allow me to call your attention to
the magnificent Gateway of India that you see before you.
It was erected in honor of the visit of King George the
Fifth and Queen Mary in 1911. It is in the classical
Gujarat style and it is very famous. You have heard of it, I
believe."

"Of course." Nesbitt hadn't, but he was not about to
puncture the man's legitimate local pride.

"I now direct your attention to your hotel. Is there anything about its architecture that strikes you as unusual?"

Nesbitt surveyed the structure quite carefully before he
answered. "It doesn't look like any other hotel I have
seen." That was safe, he concluded while he waited for
what was coming next.

"Anything else, sir?"

"Well, to be honest, the entrance isn't as impressive as I
would have expected, considering the size of the building."

"You will be interested to know, sir, that the architect
designed a most impressive entrance to this hotel. When
his plans were completed he was forced to leave for a
period of time while construction was begun. When he
returned, he discovered that the hotel was well advanced
in construction exactly as he had designed it, but facing
the wrong way. The back was to the front and the front
was to the back — I trust that that is clear. There are two

136

versions as to what occurred next. Some say that the architect, upon seeing this disaster, committed suicide. The other, which is believed to be the truth, is that he attempted suicide but fortunately without success. At any rate, the hotel was built reversed as you see. The present management claims that no mistake was made — you may judge for yourself on this point."

"It looks backwards to me," Nesbitt said.

"It also looks backwards to the rest of India; now that you are here we consider you one of us. Shall we proceed inside?"

Nesbitt walked through the building until he reached the reception lobby, which was located at the rear. There he registered and received the usual greetings. An elevator, which also faced the rear, took him up several floors where a team of bellboys and porters installed him in his room with full protocol. He gave each of them a rupee and then settled down to the business of washing up. The water taps were in good repair and while the water was not cold, it sufficed to refresh his face and hands. After he had done that, he showered and put on fresh, lighter clothing.

He was in India now, the land he had long wanted to visit. It was fully as hot as he had been led to expect, in fact even hotter, but he felt that he would be able to handle the temperature without too much trouble. His room was air-conditioned and there was a carafe of cold water provided for him together with a set of glasses carefully wrapped in paper. He helped himself to some and found it most refreshing. Now, he decided, if people would only leave him alone, he might be able really to enjoy his visit to India.

At that moment his phone rang. He picked it up to find out what it was that the management desired of him; no one else knew of his arrival.

In that, however, he was mistaken. A voice he had heard before came over the instrument. "Welcome to India, Mr. Nesbitt. I hope that you had a nice flight."

"I didn't quite catch who this is."

"George Smith, Mr. Nesbitt, and I believe that the time has come when we should have a little talk together."

9

"I UNDERSTAND that this is your first visit to India," Smith said.

"Yes, it is," Nesbitt answered.

They had met in the grill room of the hotel as casually as any two business acquaintances might have done, ready to discuss sales quotas for the coming month. Only one detail caught Nesbitt's attention: despite the fact that there were only two of them, they had been given a particularly choice table which was set in a corner by itself. No one else had been put even adjacent to them and unless the grill became very crowded indeed, probably no one would be. It was another bit of evidence that Smith carried a definite level of authority despite the fact that relations between India and the United States were not at their best, a result of the administration's backing of Pakistan during the Bangladesh campaign.

To be absolutely sure, Nesbitt put a question. "I presume it's safe for us to talk here?"

"Definitely," Smith assured him. "I'm quite sure we won't be disturbed or overheard." He picked up the menu which lay on the table before him. "How long are you planning on being in the country?"

"Just under three weeks."

"Then I suggest that you have a good dinner here while you can. There are very few places in India where you can get beef because of the prevailing religion and not everyone has a great taste for curry."

During the next five minutes they were occupied with ordering. Nesbitt noted that the waiter did not present himself until he had been signaled. That small fact could be significant, or it might mean nothing at all.

As soon as they were alone once more, Smith continued. "In view of certain recent events, there are a few things which it might be advisable for you to know now. Also, there are some questions I would like to have you answer for me if you're able."

"Go ahead," Nesbitt said, knowing that Smith could take that either way.

Smith brought his hands together on top of the table. "Naturally, for some time we have been quite familiar with your writings. They're entertaining, there's no question about that, but you also show a considerable amount of insight into the intelligence business. How did you acquire that background?"

"Very simply," Nesbitt answered him. "There's hardly

any subject in the world about which you can't learn a great deal if you're willing to make a reasonable effort. That includes intelligence work among other things. I don't know how familiar you are with literary research, but there is a tremendous amount of material that's quite open to the public and available in most good libraries. There must be fifty fairly recent books on espionage. A great deal of the history of the OSS is on record, instances of specific operations such as *The Man Who Never Was*. There's Kirkpatrick's book on the CIA, Fletcher Pratt's *Secret and Urgent*, Kahn's *The Code Breakers*, and a great many more. Actually, I believe myself that in the general field of classified information, ninety percent of all of it could be made public with no loss. It's the remaining small portion that has to be kept hidden. But if you make it a point to read everything significant that comes out, by responsible writers, that is, you can probably piece together half of the remaining ten percent."

"You must do a lot of reading," Smith commented.

"I do. I have to if I want to be accurate and make my stuff believable. There isn't any other route."

"I agree with much of that," Smith said. "I'll go a little farther and say that a great deal has been published that in my opinion never should have been. The Pratt book, for instance. When it first came out, it created some problems, I've been told."

The waiter arrived with soup and the conversation stopped while it was served. Smith tried his and then continued. "Now about yourself; do you recall writing a letter something more than a year ago to one of the branches of the government? A letter in which you were kind enough to offer your services if they were ever needed?"

"Of course, and it was probably a mistake, I recognize that now. I had come across a reference to the fact that British Intelligence made substantial use of many of England's best-known writers during World War Two. I don't flatter myself as to my abilities, but it occurred to me to write and I did. I got a very courteous brush-off reply."

"I know that you did; a lot of people are misled into believing that the business is very glamorous and romantic and they see it as a means of escape from routine. Quite a few write in as a result. In your case, knowing who you were, we went a little farther and set up a file."

"A dossier?"

"That would be too strong a word; I'd rather say that we kept you in mind. When I met you in Vienna I asked you point-blank if you were still willing to cooperate with us and you said, 'of course.' Do you recall that?"

"Certainly."

Smith paused and seemed somewhat relieved. "I'm very glad of that," he said, "because as of the present moment, things have gotten a little out of hand."

Nesbitt said nothing; he contented himself with his soup, eating it quietly and waiting for Smith to continue. After a considerable pause, he did.

"Mr. Nesbitt, in the vast, complicated structure of international politics, I believe that you recognize there are essentially two sides. Most of the major powers are in one camp or the other, and many of the lesser ones as well."

"Such as Albania."

"A good example. Now whether you personally happen to credit the fact or not, a very high percentage of the aggression that has been upsetting the world lately has been coming from what we call 'the other side.' That includes military aggression, propaganda, and subversion. It's not all one-sided, but the major efforts have been coming from them."

"I know that," Nesbitt said. "I've done five books on the subject."

"So you have, and good ones too. Now one of the jobs which occupies us is keeping track of the opposition and what they are up to. In plain language, counterespionage. Therefore we knew about a certain agent whom we code-named Feodor. He is, or was, very dangerous and was a known killer who preferred the use of a knife. We almost had him once, but he slipped away from us."

"Is he Russian?" Nesbitt asked.

"I don't know, but I doubt it; he could have come from anywhere. We had lost track of him for the time being, then he had the acute misfortune to encounter you in Berlin. Can you imagine the shock it gave us when we learned that, despite the fact that he was armed with his favorite weapon, you apparently took him bare-handed and left him in a condition where he was all but helpless?"

"How did you know it was me?" Nesbitt asked.

Smith looked at him. "We don't need to go into that. We had some very hurried conferences with the German police and, quite frankly, we weren't entirely able to convince them that you weren't one of our most effective agents. We weren't convinced either."

"I don't quite follow that."

"We're not the only players in the game, there are several other organizations whose work runs roughly parallel to ours. So now I have a question to put to you."

Nesbitt took his careful time. "If I were some kind of an agent," he said, "the chances are I wouldn't tell you or anyone else. But whether you choose to believe it or not, I have no official connections whatsoever."

Smith nodded. "That is the information I had, but there could have been an oversight somewhere. I know that you've studied karate for many years. You must be very good."

"No, not really. I do it mostly for exercise and also so that I can be accurate in describing Mark Day in action." He thought for a moment. "The incident in Berlin was the first time that I actually used it seriously."

"You picked the right time." He beckoned to the waiter who was poised just out of earshot waiting for permission to serve the main course.

After the food was on the table, Smith continued. "While you were out sightseeing that afternoon in Berlin, we talked to Washington and on the basis of your having previously offered to help us out, we made some decisions."

"I would have appreciated being consulted," Nesbitt said.

"I can understand that, my apologies. Now look at it from our viewpoint: here is an American citizen traveling abroad who suddenly becomes the object of attention by a certain rather important agent, and we have no idea why. That opens up a long list of possibilities that would have to be checked out in a hurry."

Nesbitt considered that for a minute before he responded. "A lot of possibilities," he agreed, "particularly when you didn't know me too well."

"I'm very glad you understand. In the very limited time we had at first, we had to move very rapidly. Two major possibilities had us concerned — the first that you were

144

an entirely innocent person who somehow had attracted the enemy. In that case you might need some protection. Little did we know! The other premise was that you were indeed an agent — ours or theirs — in which case we were at once vitally interested."

As Nesbitt cut his meat, his mind was functioning. "You've got my attaché case, haven't you?" he asked.

This time Smith took a moment to think. "Tell me why you believe that," he proposed.

"Because I've just figured out what's in the case you gave me to carry instead."

"Tell me."

"First of all, I saw you with Gretel Hoffmeister, or whatever her real name is, in the lobby of the Divan. Naturally that told me a lot. She planted the case on me, along with that phony photographer."

"He's a real photographer and an excellent one. We have some very fine pictures of you now for our files."

Nesbitt continued. "It simply isn't logical that you'd use me as a messenger boy; there are too many unknowns. You couldn't forecast how I'd behave, and I might change my travel plans at any time. If you wanted a courier, you'd use one of your own."

Nesbitt paused, but Smith continued to eat and made no comment. "You know what Sherlock Holmes said: when all the possibilities but one have been eliminated, the one that remains, no matter how improbable, must be the truth. You didn't take my case simply because you fancied it. You didn't plant something on me for me to deliver somewhere. You may have wanted a look at the contents, but that didn't call for a substitution of the cases. One thing remains."

Smith looked at him, his fork held halfway to his mouth. "What?" he asked.

"A radio. Some kind of transmitter that would tell you where I am, or where the case is, at any given time. Perhaps it can be triggered like a space satellite to give a return signal on demand. With the subminiature circuitry they have now, it would be easy to conceal it in the handle and there's plenty of room in the case to put in a good long spiral antenna."

There was a very long pause during which Smith did not say a thing. Nesbitt took his own time, eating his meat and enjoying the iced tea he was having with it. Finally he broke the silence. "Do you know Inspector Franzini?"

"Yes," Smith admitted.

"Then that confirms it. There were two things I noted in my contacts with him: first, he knew altogether too much about me on short notice without having been briefed. Secondly, he found my case with astonishing speed. I thought that he might have known the regular thieves who do snatches of that kind and that he simply got lucky, but that won't hold up. For one thing, when I tried to congratulate him on his achievement, he was altogether too modest about it. He didn't want to take the credit when he certainly appeared to have it coming."

Again Smith refused to make any comment; instead he made a point of calling the waiter and getting some more coffee. When he had been served, Nesbitt decided to continue a little farther. "Now something else: you knew, because you had received my letter, that I was willing to lend a hand if you wanted to make use of me. So you could very easily have given me the other attaché case, the one I have now, and asked me to carry it instead. Instead you went to the trouble to pull a switch on me, which means two things: you weren't ready to trust me with any kind of information and I wasn't, of course, intended to discover the exchange. But I did, and called at the embassy in Vienna. That must have thrown you off the track a little."

For reasons best known to himself Smith stopped eating; he still held his fork and toyed with his food, but he seemed to have lost his appetite. Nesbitt left him alone, quietly going on with his own dinner and not offering any more of his thoughts and deductions.

Presently Smith appeared to have made up his mind about something. To give himself a little additional time he cut off a piece of meat and chewed it carefully while he looked out the window and across the waters of the Arabian Sea. When he had swallowed the food in his mouth he took some coffee and then began to speak, very quietly and without any emotion in his voice.

"Mr. Nesbitt, I believe you understand that the incident in Berlin was as much a surprise to us as it was to you. We had nothing whatever to do with it and we didn't come into the picture until it was all over. Sufficient to say that as a result of it we made a decision which we felt was necessary — because we didn't know what was going on. If it had worked out, it would have accomplished two things: it would have answered a lot of questions for us and at the same time provided you with some protection which we felt you might need."

"What you're saying is, you didn't know why Feodor had chosen to search my room."

"Exactly."

Nesbitt shook his head. "I can't help you on that; I haven't been able to figure it out. It could be a case of mistaken identity, but I rather doubt it."

"So do I. And I very much doubt if Feodor is about to tell us. To continue: normally I would not tell you this, but we did plant that attaché case on you, both for your protection and also to help us in case you drew the attention of the opposition anymore. Feodor could have been checking you out for some reason of his own and that could have been the end of it. We know now that it wasn't."

"I was followed in Prague," Nesbitt said.

"We know, and that balcony trick you used was reasonably good under the circumstances. We had you covered, you see, but fortunately nothing happened."

There were two major questions that remained in Nesbitt's mind, one of which, for personal reasons, he feared to ask. He put the other one first. "Where do we go from here?"

Smith became more decisive. "We've definitely agreed that we've got to get you out of this. It isn't properly your game and you've been taking some very high risks that we simply can't allow to continue. There are two routes that we can go: one is to recommend to you very strongly that you terminate your present tour and get back home immediately. We'll send someone with you until you're safely back stateside. After that we'll still keep an eye out for you as long as seems desirable."

"No," Nesbitt responded. "I've waited too long for this trip and it's part of my business; I've got to know the backgrounds about which I write."

"There's a second alternative: we will arrange to steal your case from you in such a way that the opposition will know that you don't have it any longer. You can unload it first, so you will still have all of the contents. Then buy something locally to replace it — we'll pay for it."

Nesbitt considered that. "It might work very well, especially if it's the case they're after."

"Of course," Smith added, "we'll continue to keep a watchful eye on you, particularly after what happened in Istanbul. We had a man on you, but somehow he lost you. After this we'll use a box or whatever we consider necessary." He looked at Nesbitt rather carefully. "That doesn't imply that we think of you as incapable of taking care of yourself. On the contrary, your performance in the Grand Bazaar was incredible. You must know that."

"I was fortunate."

"That you were, but your own resourcefulness was worthy of Mark Day in his finest moment. That's about as far as I can go. If there was a real Mark Day, I'd believe it was him rather than you."

Nesbitt passed that off. "There's one more thing I've got to ask you. The girl who is . . . posing as Celestine Van Damm. I take it that she is one of your people."

Smith looked at him in real surprise. "No, absolutely not. I've been going on the assumption that she was your regular girl friend who you've been writing into your books."

"She isn't. I just met her for the first time in Vienna. Well — almost."

"Perhaps you'd better tell me about it." Smith leaned forward to listen.

Nesbitt did. "What it amounts to," he concluded, "is that she's too good to be real. She's exactly the person I've been writing about. That story that we had met several years ago while she was in her late girlhood sounded fine when she told it, but it may very well be one of those things that you think you recall when you actually don't — you just respond to the suggestion."

"Could you have been keeping her subconsciously in your mind without realizing it?"

Almost sadly Nesbitt shook his head. "I doubt that."

Smith let the waiter refill his water glass while he thought. "I have one explanation," he offered as soon as they were alone.

"And so have I — the same one, I believe."

"Go ahead."

Nesbitt hated to, but he refused to stick his head into the sand. "She belongs to the other side," he said.

After a full night's rest that he badly needed, Ed Nesbitt set out on a tour of Bombay. He tried to absorb its atmosphere as he listened to his guide, but he could not help trying to pick up some evidence of an invisible escort that was probably out there somewhere. It was even possible that he had two, but he saw nothing that he could definitely identify as a tag.

After lunch at the hotel, during which he did some further hard thinking, he tried the Taj Mahal's public relations office. He found a young woman there who seemed interesting at sight. "Do you speak English?" he asked.

"Certainly, sir, how may I help you?"

"May I ask your name?"

"Zarine."

"Zarine, I'm Ed Nesbitt, a novelist."

"We know, sir. You are the author of the Mark Day books."

That helped a little. "I want to see something of Bombay this afternoon that isn't on the regular tourist itineraries. The inner part of the city. Can you help me?"

Zarine could; she picked up a telephone and held a conversation in a language that was completely remote from anything Nesbitt had ever heard. After three or four minutes she hung up. "A car will be here for you in fifteen minutes," she said. "It will have a special driver and a special guide. The guide understands what it is that you want and he believes that he can be helpful."

Nesbitt thanked her and returned to the lobby. There, with the help of the assistant manager, he put his traveler's checks, airline tickets, and accumulated notes in the hotel safe. If he lost his case now, nothing of real importance to him would be gone. He washed up and waited for the car to arrive.

The afternoon was one of the best of his trip. He saw the open-air laundry that is peculiar to Bombay, a Parsee fire temple from the outside, the park where the Towers of Silence were located, and then the obviously nontourist flea market. He spent two hours there, going from stall to stall, taking in the merchandise and the types of people who swarmed through the market in the near-stifling heat. Against this setting he could write rich and pungent copy that would really involve his readers and he was in his element. He added substantially to his notes and put all other thoughts as far out of his mind as he could manage.

That evening he dined by invitation with the hotel manager and attended a performance of Indian dances. He retired early, satisfied with his day.

In the morning he caught a very early flight to New

151

Delhi and checked in at the Oberei with everything in order. In the afternoon his conventional tour of the city was uninterrupted. By the time that he sat down to have his dinner it seemed as if the clouds had blown away and his life had returned completely to normal.

He took the attaché case with him the next day when he climbed into a hire car early in the morning headed for Agra. Once again he had taken the precaution of emptying it of all its important contents. He rode through the intense heat across the face of North Central India until he reached Agra. Ten minutes' drive through the city took him to a busy parking lot. From there he passed through the huge red gateway that served as an entrance and then stopped in his tracks for a long while as he beheld the spectacle of the Taj Mahal.

For the first time on his trip he put aside all thought of Mark Day, of future books, or of the remarkable events that had been happening, in order to yield himself up to the timeless spell of the incomparable tomb. Almost in respectful awe, he allowed himself to be guided up to and through the marble miracle; when he had done that he dismissed his guide and simply let the wonder of the world that so speaks from the heart of India completely engulf him. When he had seen it from every available angle he found a place to sit beside the reflecting pool and tried to make himself one with where he was and what he was seeing. Only one outside thought reached through to him; he forgot himself momentarily and wished that Celestine Van Damm could be there to share this profound experience with him. Then he remembered.

When at last he turned his back on the Taj and slowly returned to where his car was still waiting, he knew that the whole trip, with all of its unexpected hazards, had been and was worth far more than its cost in time and money.

As he was entering the outskirts of Delhi on the return trip the attaché case was expertly stolen from his car. He had noted another vehicle behind his own which had been following for some blocks, but he had assumed that it was someone else returning from Agra; his mind had been too full for him to pay it any special attention.

He came to when his car door was jerked open and his case seized before he could make a move. It was done so quickly he did not even get a good, careful look at the man in the white garments who snatched it and was gone somewhere in the milling mass of humanity that crowded both sides of the narrow roadway. Nesbitt's first instinct was to attempt pursuit; he jumped from the car and tried to follow, but he realized almost at once that it was impossible. The thief knew the area — that was obvious — and Nesbitt did not. He put on a convincing show of frustration and rage and then returned to his waiting car.

The driver said nothing to him; probably he understood no English. When they reached the hotel Nesbitt went immediately to the assistant manager's desk, told his brief story, and asked that the police be advised. He did not overdo it, but if anyone in the lobby happened to be interested, it was quite clear what was going on.

The assistant manager deeply regretted what had happened and offered every assistance within his power. The police were notified. At dinner Nesbitt was careful to mention to the headwaiter who seated him that he was expecting a possible call because of his loss. That was enough, he had spread a sufficiently rich trail that could not be missed by the opposition — anything more might give away the fact that it was a plant.

After dinner he drifted into the cocktail lounge hoping for a contact. He picked his location carefully and felt that Day himself could not have done better. He ordered and then sat quietly, reviewing in his mind the role he was now playing. He was confident that he was on the track so far; the case even contained some raw notes and other jottings which would make it look entirely genuine if by any chance someone not in on the game were to examine the contents. As a matter of fact the notes were entirely bona fide and there was no way that anyone could know that he had carefully copied them the night before.

"Mr. Nesbitt?"

He had been so wrapped up in his thoughts that he had not even seen the man who had approached him. He was obviously an Indian, well-dressed in a local suit, clean white shirt, and a narrow black tie. His dark features were just like so many thousands of others Nesbitt had already seen in India, but he liked the man nevertheless — he had an air of courtesy and good manners about him that meant something.

"What can I do for you?" Ed asked.

"This is an imposition, sir, but since you are actually here in Delhi — is it too much to ask if you will sign a book for me?" As he spoke he held out one of Nesbitt's recent titles in the British edition.

"I'll be happy to," Nesbitt said. "Please sit down."

He opened the volume to the title page, then took out a brush pen and uncapped it. "To whom shall I make it?" he asked.

154

His visitor leaned slightly forward. "To Mr. George Smith."

Nesbitt held the pen poised, thinking hard. "And what is your name?" he asked.

"It doesn't matter, sir."

"Have you seen Mr. Smith recently?"

"Quite recently, yes, sir."

Since it was the only thing to do, Nesbitt wrote in the book *Very Sincerely* and signed his name. Then he closed it and handed it over. "I've lost my attaché case," he remarked. "It was stolen from me this afternoon."

"I have heard, sir, and I am very sorry for your loss."

"Perhaps I may get it back sometime."

Once more the young Indian leaned forward and dropped his voice still further. "That is possibly in doubt, sir. You see, it was not our people who took it."

10

BEFORE THE SUN had reached a point thirty degrees above the horizon, its torrid heat had already infused the incredibly crowded, dirt clogged, cow-infested city of Calcutta. On the unshaded sidewalks endless thousands of Indians stood, sat, or lay down, for the moment content merely to exist; on the crumbling streets a profusion of loincloth-clad runners pulled their rickshaws, their insensitive bare feet enduring the blistering heat of the asphalt, the stones and debris, the animal dung, and the many patches of garbage as they dodged the heavy motor traffic, trying by the racking of their bodies to earn enough to avoid starvation.

Streetcars lumbered their way, with more passengers clinging to their outsides than were crammed inside. On the buildings high above, huge billboards promoted new Indian motion pictures with broad, garish displays; below them the jammed traffic was complicated even more by the wandering, homeless cows who had no chance whatsoever to find fodder where they were and who did not know how to escape from the fearful, man-made jungle in which they found themselves entrapped.

In the air-conditioned tourist shops, English-speaking, sari-clad girls displayed jewelry, sandalwood carvings, ivories from Jaipur, silks, and papier-maché products from Kashmir to customers who were quickly served with complimentary iced drinks to keep them from leaving and to put them under implied obligation to buy.

In the lobby of the Grand Hotel, which offered isolation from the surrounding squalor for those who could afford it, another unexpected power failure was allowing the outside heat to flow in like an unseen tidal wave charged with mixed odors and other evidences of the harsh realities that existed just outside the protected entranceway. In uncomfortable suits the clerks behind the desks maintained appearances and offered apologies whenever they were indicated. In the very large dining room Ed Nesbitt sat by himself, eating slowly as he reviewed in his mind the many experiences he had crowded into the past several days. On the floor directly beside his chair he had the barely adequate attaché case he had bought in Delhi after his other one had been stolen.

He had seen many things since that event had occurred. He had been to Benares where he had watched the faithful Hindus purifying themselves in the muddy waters of the sacred Ganges. At Sarnath he had visited the place where the Lord Buddha had preached His first sermon after His

157

enlightenment. At Jaipur he had been dazzled by the pink city and the fabulous palace he had climbed a considerable hill to see. Now he was in Calcutta to rest for a day or two before setting out for fabled Darjeeling and the ride that he had promised himself on the most incredible railroad in the world — the toy train of the Himalaya.

That is, if everything went well.

During the past week and a half he had been expecting trouble at any moment. The snatching of his attaché case in Delhi had been a professional heist — the man who had grabbed it had known exactly what he was after and he had not wasted a fraction of a second. The opposition had it, and in their eyes the secret radio it contained would be proof positive that he was an American agent and therefore a definite target to be eliminated. They had already tried it once and he had no doubt that they would try again.

He was certain about the radio. The more he reviewed his deduction concerning its existence, the stronger it became in his mind. Also, when he had told George Smith about his conclusion, that elusive gentleman had said nothing, which was in itself significant.

Somewhere, presumably, he still had an escort of Smith's people, but he had not been able to spot even one of them since he had left Delhi. If they were still covering him they were certainly good, for he had set a fast pace that would automatically have made their job many times more difficult.

Several times he had considered taking Smith's suggestion and heading for home — it was unquestionably the only prudent thing to do. He was not being paid to take the risks that belonged to a secret agent and he knew in his own heart that he was not qualified to handle them. He had been extraordinarily lucky twice, but he couldn't expect that to continue.

At the known risk of being foolhardy he had elected to stay with his original schedule for one determined reason: he didn't like the idea of being made to run and hide. Mark Day would never have done such a thing for a moment and while he was certainly not Day, he himself held many of the same positions that his fictional hero espoused.

For perhaps the twentieth time he quietly rationalized that he was not taking any undue chances. The opposition had the case, and that was what they had been after. Smith was covering him, he had been told that. Nothing whatever had happened to him of an untoward nature since he had left Delhi more than ten days ago. As long as he kept his mind on that path and that path alone, it all seemed very reasonable and right. Unfortunately his intelligence intervened and told him in definite terms that this optimistic reasoning was invalid. He had going for him Smith's cover, if it was still in place, and that was just about all. A sharp chill ran down his spine and he could not shake it off.

A waiter he had not seen approaching drew out a chair at his table and gestured. As Nesbitt looked up he had a sudden need to control himself: Celestine Van Damm was about to be seated beside him.

The bubble of false confidence burst as he rose to his feet. He knew who she was now, and that fact alone told him that the opposition was still definitely interested in his movements. They had put her in again and the game was very much afoot.

"Surprise!" Celestine said. She pulled up her chair, rested her elbows on the table, and favored him with a bright smile.

Nesbitt sat down and tried to think with the speed of Mark Day, but without success. "I was looking for you in Jaipur," was all that he could manage.

"I was delayed."

"First of all," he began once more, "have you eaten?"

"A little."

"Have some more." He signaled to a waiter.

After Celestine had ordered a fruit salad and iced tea, she took over the conversation. "This may come as a shock to you," she said, "but I do have things to do occasionally. I've actually been quite busy."

Damn right, Nesbitt thought.

"Anyhow, it's all over now for a while and I can resume my pose as a young woman of leisure." She folded her hands under her chin. "Venice is a wonderful place, but you added something to it that it never had before — something I found pretty exciting. In the city and . . ." She looked carefully at him, ". . . in bed."

"I was inspired," Nesbitt said.

"Europe is full of engaging men," Celestine continued, taking her time. "Some of them are not quite as engaging as they think they are, but on the whole there is a very good choice. A single girl can usually find a suitable escort quite easily, especially if the impression is current that she has a few bucks in the bank." She paused again while she shaped her words. "As of now you have the whole stable of them outclassed, and by that I don't mean that I've tried them all out — I can usually tell just by looking."

Ed said nothing, but his thoughts were legion. He would

160

have practically sold his soul to have been able to believe her, but he knew better. He knew who she really was, and he was more than aware of his own limitations. The gulf between himself and Mark Day was wider than it had ever been before.

"Incidentally," Celestine went on, "quite a few times I've been able to get rid of troublesome men by telling them that if I went with someone else, Mark Day wouldn't like it. You have no idea how effective that is, they melt away like magic."

"Do they really buy it?" Nesbitt asked.

"They most certainly do. After all, Van Damm isn't that common a name, you know."

That reminded him again, but at the same time he had to admire her nerve; she had called a strike on herself without turning a hair.

The waiter arrived with glasses of ice water which spared Ed from having to say anything. He did not trust himself to speak, but there was a multitude of things about which he was glad to be able to remain silent.

Celestine sipped the fresh water and mercifully changed the topic. "Where are you going from here?" she asked.

Nesbitt reached for his own water glass to give himself time to think. He put the pieces together quickly: she had found him here so obviously she was familiar with his movements or could learn them easily. His schedule was practically an open book with all of the reservations that had been made for him, therefore he might as well tell her.

He put down the glass. "I'm going to Darjeeling," he said. "I've always wanted to see it, I understand that it's fabulous. And I want to ride that wonderful train. It's like a toy, the gauge is only two feet and everything else is scaled way down, but it's still a real, live, fire-spitting, mountain-climbing, cinder-flinging railroad that's the number one attraction in India after the Taj. Unfortunately, they don't know it."

He was surprised by the look in Celestine's eyes. "And you're going to ride it all the way up to Darjeeling?"

"I am."

She reached her hand across the table and took his in a surprisingly firm grip. "Take me with you, I want to go!" she declared.

He saw through that as though it had been plate glass, but in the same moment he knew that there was no way he could duck it. She could go if she wanted to and there was no way he could stop her. "Why not," he said and tried to make it sound genuine.

"There's a good hotel at Darjeeling?" she asked.

"The Mount Everest. I've never seen it, but I understand that it's been there since Kipling. It should be colorful, if nothing else."

Celestine fell silent for a moment; the interval grew longer as the waiter brought the food. When he had left, she pitched her voice a little lower and spoke with a good imitation of quiet sincerity. "I don't throw myself at men," she said. "I don't have to, I think you know that."

Ed nodded.

"If you have a fault, it's that you underrate yourself too much. You've got a talent that's made you world-famous. But apart from that — strictly apart — you're one hell of a guy."

"No I'm not," Nesbitt said.

"Which proves my point."

Celestine toyed with a bit of banana for a second before

she put it into her mouth. When she was ready, she spoke again. "Harry Truman wasn't tall, dark, and handsome, Ben Franklin was fat, Lincoln was all but hopeless when he was forced into a marriage he didn't want, and I could go on. There's nothing wrong with your appearance, your body, or your brain. That's as far as I'm going to go, now you pick up the ball the way that you're supposed to — you know how."

Nesbitt made a decision. He knew that she was good — she was superb — and probably as dangerous as a woman could be. Fully aware of all that, he went ahead anyway.

"After a day's rest, if anyone can rest in Calcutta, I'm going up into the Himalaya. By air to Bagdogra, then by that incredible train up from the plains of India. Up through the tea plantations, up through the clouds to Darjeeling where you can stand and see right in front of you the incomparable splendor of Kanchenjunga soaring in one gigantic massif up to and beyond twenty-eight thousand feet and know that you are finally at the far and absolute end of the earth. That's what I'm going to do. I'm going to have dinner, presumably at the Mount Everest, and after an evening of whatever there is to do up there, I'm going to go to bed and dream vast and wonderful tales about the roof of the world. Now the question is, do you want to come and share this with me?"

"Yes!" Celestine said, her eyes fixed on him. "All of it."

He finished his glass of water because he was still thirsty. "Then pack," he told her.

The 737 northbound from Calcutta was crowded to capacity. As the miles slid behind, it passed towering cumulus clouds that gave evidence of a frontal passage and threatened to grow into mighty thunderheads before the day was done. Eventually it let down, picking its way until it was skimming low over the baked flat ground and then touching down on a runway barely adequate to handle it.

In the terminal building that was not much larger than a small house there were additional formalities to go through. Special permission had to be obtained to go to Darjeeling because of its proximity to Bhutan, Sikkim, and Communist China. After more than thirty minutes of standing in a sweltering, almost immobile line they at last signed the book in which they were required to give all pertinent information and reclaimed their baggage.

A travel agent equipped with a smattering of English was there to meet them. He hurried them into one of the inevitable Ambassador cars while their baggage was being crammed in back and wherever else it would go. The moment that had been done the driver took off as best he could across the open country; the airport seemed to have been built in lonesome isolation miles from any visible destination. As the car lurched its way over the uncertain road, the guide explained about the train. "It is too late we make start, but we catch — little farther."

Nesbitt assessed once more the limited powers of the car and asked, "Can we catch it?"

"Oh yes, yes. Maximum speed of train, eight miles per hour." The guide said that with the assurance of a memorized phrase and Ed detected it.

"Do many people take the train?" he asked.

"Many people, yes, sahib. But all Indian people. Little foreigners. Few come, they take taxi."

The car plowed on, born like so many other natives of

India for only a limited existence, but doing its feeble best. Presently alongside the road there were railroad tracks like those common in amusement parks, but laid with stronger steel. The gauge was so narrow it was ludicrous. Nesbitt looked ahead and saw, perhaps a mile ahead of them, a short pillar of smoke that could be the locomotive.

The toy train of the Himalaya! Nesbitt was a grown man, mature and well in possession of himself, but for just a moment his long eclipsed boyhood lived again as he savored this new and unique adventure. The taxi was doing almost forty miles an hour; the road had improved somewhat. If the train was indeed limited to eight miles per hour, then the rate of closure was quite satisfactory and they would catch it shortly.

When they did it was chugging its way with all of the dignity and determination of a great Rocky Mountain articulated in the supreme days of steam power. The stocky, miniature locomotive was pulling a string of not more than five cars that were scaled down like itself. Then the train was behind them as the taxi hurried on as best it could toward the next station ahead.

It was not far, but when they arrived there they had plenty of time to accept the tickets that the travel agent bought for them, watch their luggage being unloaded, and then stand for a little while on the platform beside the absurdly narrow roadbed. On a siding a boxcar that appeared to be approximately nine feet long stood patiently waiting for an assignment. Down the tracks the pillar of smoke and steam was drawing closer.

The train pulled in and stopped, quite unaware that it was not the Twentieth Century Limited. It lacked severely in almost everything but dignity, but it seemed aware that

165

it was the only train of its kind in the world and that it was immune to competition. Nesbitt helped Celestine into the first-class car and then followed himself. It was miniature, of course, with two facing benches running down each side and in the center a small closed compartment which made its purpose known by an undeniable odor that the wide-open windows could not completely suppress.

Their baggage was piled on, they were wished well, and the train started. There were four others in the coach, all Indians who nodded and offered their goodwill despite the language barrier. Celestine responded with bewitching smiles all around; in less than a minute she had them all at her feet and Nesbitt found himself the target of looks of congratulation, understandable envy, and awareness of the separation of the other riders from this unattainable beauty from another world. There was no resentment, only acceptance which, to Nesbitt, made it more tragic still.

The little car swayed gently from side to side for the next twenty minutes while ahead a majestic panorama of mountains crept closer. Then trees began to appear and the start of a small gully. The straight roadbed commenced to turn and the tiny engine could be heard putting forth more effort. The curves gradually tightened until they were astonishing, but the little train bent itself nearly double and negotiated them, one directly after another. Presently there was a momentary viewpoint and the vast hot plain lay visibly below.

Without the aid of cogs the miniature train continued to climb, bending incessantly from one sharp turn into another, sometimes in forest, frequently on the very edge of a growing downward plunge. It crossed and recrossed a roadway, once three times within two hundred feet. Then, in the middle of a steep upward slope, the track ended, a resolute bumper marking the visible end of the line. Behind the last car someone threw a switch; moments later the train went into reverse, backing its way up a switchback for a half mile or more. Another change of direction took it forward once again, now a good bit higher than it had been at the start of the maneuver. A waterfall came into view and the locomotive stopped for water.

For almost six hours Ed Nesbitt drank in the experience, disregarding the flow of cinders, the rocking of the coach, and the other minor irritations. His enjoyment was enriched by the spirit of adventure that Celestine displayed without reserve; she seemed to delight in every fresh facet of the trip and at the frequent stops she always was first off to watch the raking of the ashes from the firebox, to smile at the children that swarmed about her, and to enjoy the increasingly spectacular views. By now the mountain they were on loomed stark and mighty above them, giving the illusion that each fresh viewpoint would reveal new and greater vaulting heights, with more yet to come.

Nesbitt had to admire her — the way that she resisted any evidence of fatigue or flagging interest in the adventure. As for himself, the toy train was all that he had expected it to be and a good deal more in the bargain. He drank in every moment of the trip, even the three times that the train ran under a short viaduct, looped completely around, and then crossed its own tracks by means of the bridge it had just been under. Clouds began to drift alongside them and the thin fine mist could actually be felt inside the narrow little car. At the occasional breaks that came, a rich panorama of hillside tea plantations rewarded them as with tireless energy the little train chugged higher and higher, apparently aware that it was going where none of the wide-gauge monarchs would ever dare to venture. It clung to the very edge of sheer cliff faces and skidded its wheels occasionally where the rails were wet from the clouds and a thin mist of rain.

When at last they broke out above the cumulus, the sun hung just atop the mountains immediately to the west. Its last illumination was in the sky as the stout little engine, snorting its triumph, reached level ground at last and whistled its way into the Darjeeling station where it came to rest.

"Did you like it?" Nesbitt asked.

"It was fantastic," Celestine answered. "I like my creature comforts, but I wouldn't have missed that ride for anything I know on earth. All I can say is, thank you."

For a moment Nesbitt wanted desperately to believe in her; if he only could, he felt that he would have been able to go out and walk on the tops of the clouds that were spread out like a vast cotton blanket across the wide valley of indefinite depth below them. He held himself in check with an effort, determined to reveal no hint of what he knew. Out of the gathering darkness a man approached him and addressed him by name — the tourist service was on the job even up here.

The Mount Everest Hotel was a monolith of sorts itself; it took a stiff climb on foot to reach it where it hung like a medieval fortress on the steep side of a slope that vanished upward into the mist. Nesbitt had never seen a hotel where the guests had to exert themselves like that to reach the lobby. He felt the thinness of the air and his breath was short when he finally held open the door for Celestine to step inside. As he followed her, he was greeted by a

168

candle-lit dimness and a suggestion of otherworldliness that made his fertile mind think at once of the Castle Dracula.

The receptionist behind the modest counter brought him back to reality. "Good evening, Mr. Nesbitt, sir. Welcome to the Mount Everest. We are greatly honored to have you here; we have been expecting you."

"Thank you," Nesbitt said as he picked up the pen to write.

"Excuse me, Mr. Nesbitt, do I understand correctly that we are also to entertain Miss Celestine Van Damm?"

"You do," Ed answered.

The clerk was clearly awed. "At the Oxford Book Shop, sir, we found two books by you. We have all read them. We are overwhelmed, sir. And Miss Van Damm herself — I can hardly believe it."

Nesbitt finished writing his name. He had hesitated a bare moment just before doing so, but the passports they carried would not have allowed of any fiction as to their relationship. He handed the pen to Celestine.

For the first time he saw her writing: strong, firm, and oddly slanted, but entirely legible. He knew nothing of graphology, but he knew that the style she used fitted her perfectly. Inwardly he kept wishing that she would make just one mistake and betray herself again, it would have done much to relieve the unceasing mental pressure he was under.

Celestine spoke to the clerk. "We do not wish it generally known that we are married. Can you arrange it?"

"Miss Van Damm, of course. I will even show that you are in separate rooms on our records. Please excuse the fact that there is no power; on alternate days it goes to the other side of the valley. Tomorrow there will be lights here,

169

but only at half strength. We have only limited resources in Darjeeling."

"I think it's very romantic," Celestine said. "When will dinner be served?"

"At your convenience — perhaps in an hour?"

"That will be fine."

Two porters materialized from somewhere and shouldered the baggage; after that the trek began. The clerk led the way through a darkened immense lobby, up a wide double staircase into a ballroom which was obviously unused, then down a long corridor, up a narrow set of steps where lighted candles tilted at dangerous angles on the newel posts, down another corridor, around a corner, and down a short passageway where he unlocked a door.

It was actually a suite and probably the best that the establishment had to offer. The sitting room had a series of windows facing the west and a fireplace so tiny and shallow it seemed barely six inches deep and hardly more than a foot wide. A small pile of wood beside it proved that it was indeed intended for use. There was a bathroom of sorts, but to Ed any sort of a bathroom in Darjeeling had to be considered a plus. The bedroom had ample space, another of the oddly shaped fireplaces, and a double bed that offered some prospects of comfort.

As soon as the baggage had been put down, the two porters went to work building fires designed to fit the limited dimensions while the clerk made a show of adjusting the window shades. "We will have hot water for you in a little while," he promised. "It is not like the city, but we will do our best. Please be comfortable." He waved the porters out before Nesbitt could tip them and retreated himself, closing the door behind him.

It was the first time in his life that Nesbitt had ever checked into a hotel with a woman who was not his wife. He was not a saint, but because he was prominent and his name was well-known, he had to be unusually careful. Or so it had always seemed.

Celestine came to him, turned him around, and kissed him. "How does it feel to be my husband?" she asked.

He took her and held her. "I can't tell you that," he answered truthfully.

She put her head on his shoulder and held him almost fiercely. "You don't know," she said, "you just don't know how much of a man you are."

She let go of him then as if she sensed that he did not believe her. Taking a small cosmetic case, she disappeared into the bathroom. He waited a moment after she was gone, fighting with himself, trying to force logic to conquer emotion and succeeding only partly.

He knew that he would have to change his clothes, what he had on was badly soiled from the train ride. He opened his own case and took out what he needed. When he had done that he got out of everything and put on the light dressing gown that he carried to avoid appearing any less attractive than he had to, and sat down by the window.

He could see little outside; the sky was all but dark and the mist of the clouds still shrouded what he knew had to be a spectacular view when the weather was clear. Once more, carefully and as coldly as he could, he reviewed the facts in his mind concerning the girl who was with him now. He attempted to block out his attraction to her, her willingness to share experiences with him, and the fact that she was, still almost unbelievably, his own creation dramatically come to life. Marshaling everything that he

truly knew about her, he came inevitably to the same conclusion he had before — she had to be an agent. One added
piece of information that he had been denying supplied
further proof: it took a Mark Day to capture the interest of
a girl like her — he had said precisely that during the
interview in Berlin. Despite two pieces of exceptional good
luck he was not Day and very far from that standard. Yet
she had attached herself to him and now they were
traveling together. The girl who was calling herself Celestine Van Damm could have practically any man she
wanted; there was no acceptable reason at all why she
should choose to be with him.

At that moment he desperately wanted to escape into the
fiction world of his own shaping where he could dictate the
passage of events and make things come out the right
way.

Celestine came out of the bathroom in her slip. "Your
turn," she said. "The hot water is up, but don't expect too
much — it's barely lukewarm."

Ed Nesbitt got to his feet. "I want to shower anyway,"
he told her and closed the door behind him. A certain
sense of defeat was in him and he could not shake it off.

Their entrance into the dining room was an event. Celestine looked exactly like the person she was supposed to be,
the only word he could think of to describe her was capti-
vating. The room itself was moderately small with eight or
nine candle-lit tables set and ready. A half-dozen waiters
hovered in the background; they were not as dark-skinned
as their counterparts in the major cities of India that
Nesbitt had visited and they were of stockier build, but

their manner was much the same. Everything was in readiness for the evening, but no other guests had as yet appeared.

A very young headwaiter came forward to greet them. He wore a simple black suit closely cut out of the plainest material, but it represented an effort toward formality. He bowed slightly and led them to a table in the corner of the room that had two extra candles to give a little added light. Nesbitt's deduction was swift and accurate — they were the only guests in the hotel.

As they were seated he looked across at Celestine and sensed that she knew also. Nevertheless, he was glad that she had dressed so beautifully for the occasion; it was not wasted on the staff and it was not wasted on him. As she accepted the menu she looked around the room and shared one of her loveliest smiles with all of the waiters who were gathering in the background. In so doing she won them all. That made another deduction easy: they all knew who she was, or who she was supposed to be. Ed had a moment of satisfaction — the knowledge that even at this remote hill station on the border of India, very close to the obscure small Himalayan kingdoms, his work was known and his books read.

The typed menu he was handed listed the available dinner; there was no a la carte. Even as he noted that, the headwaiter stood ready at his elbow to take his order. "The chef has prepared this for you," he said, "but if it is not satisfactory, something else can be arranged."

Nesbitt handed back the menu. "It will be fine, thank you."

"And will Miss Van Damm have the same?"

So he knew. Of course — they all would.

He looked across the table, pretending to ask her preference.

She responded flawlessly. "I would like the prepared dinner very much." She smiled at him and folded her hands under her chin, as she had a way of doing.

The meal itself was a little better than he had hoped for and the service was extravagant: each time that he took the smallest sip from his water glass it was immediately refilled. The attentive headwaiter stood like a fixed statue close by, keeping an eye on everything.

"Why don't you sit down," Nesbitt invited.

"No thank you sir — it is my duty."

When they had finished Ed signed the check and added as generous a tip as the amount would permit, then they were ushered out of the dining room with full ceremony.

As they stepped through the doorway, they were greeted by the sound of music. Miraculously, on the bandstand of the shadowy ballroom a nine-piece orchestra was assembled. The headwaiter explained as he said good-night. "They come here regularly to play. Even when there are no people they come in order to practice. It gives them pleasure."

Ed Nesbitt earned his living in the world of imagination and he knew it well. Deliberately he put out of his mind the things that he knew, and turned to his companion. "May I have this dance?" he asked.

"Of course."

The way she spoke the words was miraculous; she almost perfumed them and in so doing transformed the empty ballroom into a New Year's Gala in Vienna. And, in the eyes of Nesbitt, she became by far the most desirable partner at that extravagant, traditionally wonderful affair. A few steps took them onto the floor, then he turned and took her into his arms.

She danced like an angel, as he knew that she could. Under the crystal chandeliers of a Viennese palace they danced to the music of the great philharmonic, as the melody flowed Nesbitt held Celestine in his arms and thought of the reigning Emperor Franz Josef, of Johann Strauss, Jr., and of the immortal figure of Liszt himself who might arrive at any moment.

Somehow, by some kind of feminine alchemy, Celestine understood. She was his lady and she looked, acted, and breathed her role to perfection. They danced together, aware only of the music and themselves until the orchestra at last stopped playing. Together they walked over and gave the musicians their applause, then he offered her his arm to escort her off the floor.

The room was moderately warm when they returned; the fires had become glowing embers and the mists before the windows had cleared. They stood together and looked out, but there was little moonlight, instead the stars in a frozen shower of brilliance filled the sky. Ed opened the window and let the chill-filled mountain air come in enough to fill his lungs. He could not see the Himalaya, but he knew that they were there. Via magic carpet they were back in Darjeeling and in a region that was richly filled with its own past, traditions, and hidden mysteries.

The mind of Ed Nesbitt refused to play the tocsin any longer; it demanded respite and he granted it. He stood with his arm around the waist of Celestine Van Damm and allowed himself to drink from the cup of fulfillment. "Somehow," he said, the words forming automatically without his conscious thought, "I have the feeling that my

175

life is coming to a climax. It seems almost as if I still have to find myself, to know what is expected of me."

She leaned against him a little more until the warmth of her poured into his bloodstream. "I know," she answered. "I understand."

She turned and looked at him, her eyes meeting his depth for depth, forming a bond invisible but intense. "I think too that your life is going to reach its ultimate experience — right here in Darjeeling."

11

THEY WERE INTERRUPTED by a soft knocking at the door. When Nesbitt opened it, he discovered the receptionist who had shown them to their room. "Excuse me, sir," the man said, "but I thought I should tell you. The weather, it is clearing. Tomorrow morning there is a good chance that there will be a view from Tiger Hill. Shall I arrange the trip?"

"Tell me a little more," Ed said.

"It is necessary to get up very early. We will not call you unless it is clear, but if it is, you can see the sunrise over Mount Everest. It is one of the greatest sights in the world, sir — the Himalaya at sunrise is beyond description. Usually at this season it is too cloudy, but it may be all right in the morning."

"What time would we have to get up?"

"At four thirty, sir, but you will not regret it."

"Will we walk to the hill?"

"Oh, no, sir, it is about fifteen kilometers and it is necessary to take a Land Rover; an ordinary car could never get up the road. We can arrange it."

Nesbitt turned and looked at Celestine. "Why not," she said.

"All right, we'll go," he declared. "Make the arrangements. But don't call us if it isn't clear."

"Understood, sir. Have a good rest, sir. Good-night, sir."

Nesbitt closed the door, but before he could speak Celestine read his thoughts. "We'll have lots of time," she said, "At least I hope so."

That touched a nerve in Nesbitt, but he did not let it show. "If we're going to get up that early . . ." he began.

"Suppose you put a little more wood on the fires while I get ready."

"All right."

He did that simple chore while his heart pounded faster than it should. It could have been the altitude, but it was more likely the prospect of what lay immediately before him — or possibly the mental reservations that had been dogging him so persistently. He turned off the lights, relying on the glow from the fires to show the location of objects in the near darkness. Then he undressed and stood once more looking out of the window — thinking.

When Celestine came out of the bathroom he went in, splashed water over his face, and brushed his teeth. As he looked into the mirror he saw once more the fragments of the shattered marriage that had torn him apart many years before. He had tried to wash that permanently out

178

of his mind, but the two years during which it had lasted still had the power to torture him, sometimes when he allowed it to, more frequently when he did not.

He finished, turned off the light, and came out into the sitting room. He did not really care whether the hotel believed that they were married or not — it didn't matter that much. He looked into the darkness, his eyes adjusting themselves for the first few seconds. Then he saw Celestine standing by the window where he had been, and his breath caught for a moment in his throat. He had somehow visualized finding her in some filmy negligee tied at the throat and falling in wide unbroken folds, but she needed no such enticements — she was perfectly nude and any kind of clothing would have detracted from her. He sensed, and understood, that she was well beyond the nineteenth century's fear-inspired standards of concealment. She quite simply acknowledged that she was a female and made no pretense that she was in some mystical way physically different from all of the millions of others. Nesbitt knew that she was not trying to tempt him; there was no need. She was completely natural and he accepted that gratefully. God, if he could really have a woman like her!

He stood beside her for a few moments. He had nothing to say: he was content just to be with her — thrusting out of his mind the secret knowledge that was lurking there. Fate to some extent was taking a hand now in the affairs of his life and he knew that it was his role to ride for a while in whichever direction he was carried.

"Let's go to bed," Celestine said.

It was a little uncomfortable at first between the sheets,

but such external considerations quickly took flight. Celestine's warm and gentle body next to his transported Nesbitt to Elysium and at last broke the grip of his nagging mind. He took her to him, kissed her, held her, and wondered why his God was being so wonderfully good to him.

The fires had burned down to partially glowing ashes when he was awakened by knocking on the door. "All right, thank you," he called and knew that he had been understood when the sound ceased. He turned to wake Celestine, but she was already struggling to sit up beside him. Despite the drugged state of his mind he allowed himself to kiss her once more before he put his feet down on the thin carpet and began to look for his clothes.

In fifteen minutes they were ready, carrying the warmest coats they had as they made the long trek down to the lobby. There the clerk who had awakened them had hot tea waiting. "The Land Rover is here," he told them. "You are up in good time."

Nesbitt thanked him, handed a steaming cup to Celestine, and then picked up his own. It was not his choice of beverages, but it went down well and promised to fortify him against the cold outside. When they had finished, they went down the long flights of steps in the dark and climbed into the squared-off vehicle that was awaiting them. True to tradition there was a driver and a guide, a kind of work rule in its way that was probably for the best. As soon as they were both on board, the car started up and began to roll down the reasonably well-paved road.

They stayed on it for a few miles, then they turned off to the left and began to climb. Nesbitt studied the road and wondered if there was another like it in the world. It was paved after a fashion, but it had been laid out in such a way that no normal car could possibly have negotiated its steep pitch and turns of only a few feet in radius. It was a highway for specialized vehicles only; the driver of the Land Rover shifted into four-wheel drive and, as the sky began to grow less dark overhead, churned onward and upward.

When they reached the summit there was a very small parking area and a modest concrete building which served as a shelter from the wind. If they went to all the trouble to build a structure this far off the beaten path, Nesbitt thought to himself, the view must certainly be worth it.

"Sir," the guide said, "will you allow us to go back down again? We are expecting some more people."

"Go ahead," Nesbitt told him. "We're not likely to get lost."

"There is no chance, sir, if you remain right here. We shall return to you shortly. It is because other cars cannot come up this hill."

"I understand."

Since the wind was a little chill, he tried the door of the building, found it open, and ushered Celestine inside. "We might as well be comfortable," he told her, "The sky is still purple."

The interior of the summit house was a very small room with a thin scattering of chairs and little else; apparently it had been provided by the government since there was no evidence of any sort of commercial operation. With the Land Rover gone it was strangely quiet; there were no birdsongs at that height, no evidence of any kind of wildlife whatsoever.

"We seem to be alone for the moment," Celestine said. It was not a complaint, she made that clear with an intimate smile that reminded Nesbitt of the warmth of the bed they had left a short while before.

"We probably will be until the other visitors come, unless the abominable snowman decides to drop by."

He turned his attention to the sky and then to the vast vista that he knew was out there in the yielding darkness. As he continued to watch he saw first a thin line of very high clouds. He studied them for movement and light change until he realized that they were not clouds at all, but a mountain of such vast and overpowering size that he could hardly credit its existence.

"Celestine," he said, "Come and look."

In a few seconds she was at his side peering out. "My God!" she exclaimed softly, as though it was a two-word prayer.

The light was increasing and a hint of color began to appear over the tremendous, snow-covered massif that seemed to dominate all of creation. Its immensity challenged the senses to comprehend it as the gaining light invisibly drew back the curtain of the night.

He opened the door and led her outside. With the building behind them all evidence of humanity and its works was erased and they were together before a spectacle beyond anything their imaginations could have spawned.

"*Kanchenjunga.*" he said, not to her but to himself.

Edwin Nesbitt stood transfixed, so totally captured by the thing that he was seeing that even the potency of the girl by his side was forgotten. For a passing moment he felt pity for the others who were not there to see this crowning achievement of earthly creation. Then Celestine took his arm and pointed. He followed her direction and saw the black summit that protruded even higher still in the background.

"Everest, I think," she said.

With no real basis for it he knew that she was right. As he drank in the whole overpowering spectacle, he had a compelling urge to respond to it in a fitting manner — to somehow take the inspiration he was receiving and translate it into his work; to turn to his typewriter and reach for literary heights that he had never before dared to attempt.

The first narrow rays of the sun began to materialize in the lightening sky. As he stood there watching, the cold and the wind were erased; all external considerations of every kind were blocked out and he felt as if he was looking upon the face of God.

It was the greatest experience he had ever known and it demanded to be shared; he could not compress his swelling emotions solely within himself. In a state of mind he had never before known in his lifetime he turned to Celestine and as he did so, he saw the man with the gun.

It hit him like lightning crashing out of a clear sky. His blood froze and his limbs would not move. The impact was so great he could not utter a sound to either warn or protect the suddenly precious person beside him. One look at the man told him that his own time was running out very fast. He had often written about the reptile eyes of the professional killer, but he had never before seen them staring so intently into his own.

As the power of movement returned to him, he jerked his head quickly toward the nearby brush in a desperate search for cover. His wild hope died in midbreath as he saw that there were two of them — perfectly positioned so that they were totally out of his reach, yet close enough so that when they chose to fire, they would not miss. Like a trapped animal he looked the other way toward the summit shelter house and saw that a tall, thin man in some kind of a long coat was standing there watching him.

His next thought was self-condemning — he had permitted three men to close in on them and he had detected nothing until it was far too late. It was a disaster that never would have happened to the ever-alert Mark Day, but it had happened to him and it was total. The dream was over.

He still had sense enough to measure the angles of fire of the two gunmen. They were precise and accurate; they could fire at will at no risk whatever of hitting each other, but whichever way he might choose to try and move, he would be held in a totally exposed crossfire. Logic told him that any such desperate ploy was foredoomed; even the ground on which he stood offered no cover or comfort.

His hands in his pockets, the man in the doorway came forward. He was notably tall, probably a disadvantage in his trade, but he was not the kind of person to do the dirty work — he was the Fu Manchu who remained unseen until it pleased him to reveal himself: the invisible man behind so many operations. As he came closer Nesbitt studied his features, but he read nothing definite there.

A few feet from the two of them he stopped and remained still for a moment, the threat of the guns held at the ready reinforcing the absolute authority of his position. He studied Nesbitt as he might have examined a laboratory specimen; his control was so great he did not even waste a glance on Celestine. It flashed through Nesbitt's mind that perhaps he had no need to do that, he already knew her well enough.

"Go into the building," he said at last. His words were very heavily accented, but they were spoken with precision.

As Nesbitt moved to obey, he noted how the two gunmen shifted their positions to keep him at every moment in their unobstructed sights. Celestine did not seem to interest them as much, but as he walked toward the open door, he heard rather than saw that she was still keeping him company.

For a few seconds he tried to speculate on what Mark Day would do in a similar situation; he decided that even Day himself would have to obey the order. The only thing he managed to accomplish was symbolic and nothing more: as he reached the doorway, he stopped for a moment in order to allow Celestine to go in first. He was allowed to do that and he counted it a tiny and fragile victory.

"Against the wall," the tall man said. Despite his accent, it was clear that he was not one to waste a word, or an unnecessary motion. In response Nesbitt did what he had been told; he crossed the little room, reached the wall, and then turned toward the man who had entrapped him. If he was to die at that point in time, he would at least make his executioners look into his face as they fired. It would make no difference to them, but it would not be a coward's death.

The tall man in the coat removed one hand from his pockets to make a simple gesture. He did not even speak, so strong was the force of his presence Nesbitt sat down in a plain wooden chair as he had been directed. Celestine sat also, without a word, where the man had pointed. As one of the gunmen stood in the doorway, his weapon leveled at Nesbitt's chest, his partner entered the room and took up station at one side. Not for an instant did they relax the tight cover they had; even if he had had a gun of his own, Ed would have had no chance whatever even to get it into his hand. They were taking no chances with him and he knew that he was powerless.

The tall man who was directing the operation replaced his hand in his pocket and silently nodded. Nesbitt read that as the signal to kill and in that paralyzing moment he suddenly did not care for himself — he had had a good time. But Celestine . . .

Two seconds later he knew that he had guessed wrong; the gunman in the doorway handed his weapon to the tall man and then reached into his own pockets. He produced what appeared to be a considerable coil of iron wire and a small pair of cutters.

The controller spoke once more. "You are wanted for questioning."

That told Nesbitt a great deal. First, they were not to die at once on the spot. Two, that was probably a severe misfortune. He had no information to give, but that would not be believed. And he had no illusions that he would be questioned while comfortably seated in a chair with a cup of coffee at his elbow. Thirdly, they were to be taken somewhere.

If they were being kidnapped, the place for it had been well chosen; there was probably no other spot on the earth where an American tourist could go that was so close to so many borders leading into the other world. He still had no idea who his captors were; they were the opposition and that told him enough. Mark Day was reliable under torture, that was on his record, but his creator held no illusion that he could be equally as stoic when the reality came. It was worse because he could not possibly satisfy them that he was innocent and had nothing to tell. He was not bound by any solemn oaths or a signing of the Official Secrets Act, but that made no real difference because he would never willingly betray his country anyway; that was how he was made.

The gunman with the wire came and knelt at the side of his chair, well out of his partner's line of fire and at a point where even if Nesbitt had decided upon a desperation tactic he would be out of reach. Without a word he uncoiled a length of the wire, cut it off, and looped it around the right back rung of the chair top. Then he took Nesbitt's wrist in a grip so astonishingly powerful that it seemed to shut off all circulation to the hand and pressed it against the support. Ed wanted to fight back, not to yield so docilely, but his still functioning brain told him to conserve his resources because he had no chance whatever at that moment.

As the wire was twisted tighter and tighter around the tender flesh of his wrist the pain forced him to flinch, then he resolved to endure it because he knew that it would be with him for some time. He submitted to the wiring of his other wrist and knew that he was all but helpless — unless he could use his feet. To put the growing agony of the too-tight wires out of his mind he began to devise things he could do with his feet as soon as they were alone. Then he saw that his tormentor was cutting off another length of wire and he knew that his ankles too were going to be immobilized.

When the man was at last through with him he could

187

breathe and little else; the chair was well made of hardwood and securely put together; he tried secretly to force it to wiggle even slightly, but it yielded not an iota. He watched as a rabbit might watch a python as the gunman cut another length and began to work on Celestine. He saw every motion that the man made, and he noted that he gave no quarter at all because Celestine was a woman. When he had her wired to her chair, for a few seconds Nesbitt almost lost control of himself. The only recourse he had left was verbal abuse; he realized in time that that would be utterly futile and would only serve to make him even more impotent. Plus which they might decide to give him the butt of a gun straight into the mouth to shut him up. It took an effort, but he remained still and gave no external signs whatever of his precarious mental condition.

When the man had finished his work he did not bother to give it a final inspection; he knew his trade too well to require that. Any movement, no matter how slight, multiplied the pain instantly in Nesbitt's wrists and he knew that he could do nothing.

The man who had done the wiring retrieved his weapon from the tall man in the coat and with his colleague went out the doorway, his immediate job finished. The controller looked at them both for a moment, his face an expressionless blank, then he turned and followed his men. As he left, he shut the door carefully behind him. Nesbitt listened as acutely as he was able, but he heard no sounds of their leaving, no indications whatever of where they had gone, or how. They were professionals.

It was time for Mark Day to take over. Remembering his mental acrobatics in Berlin, and the inspiration he had found in Istanbul, Nesbitt shut his eyes, visualized Day with all the sharp realism he could command, and summoned his aid.

He tried so hard sweat in the form of a fine mist broke out on his brow, but for some stubborn reason Day refused to materialize. The inspiration would not jell; the ultra-resourceful, highly trained secret agent with the iron nerves and whipcord body remained an inert creature of his imagination. Ed Nesbitt was in the worst fix of his life, even worse than the ambush in the Grand Bazaar, and now even his brain was letting him down.

He knew he couldn't pull it off — it simply wouldn't come. He looked at Celestine, sitting so utterly helpless, and he spoke to her. "Does it hurt too much?"

She looked back, her features tightened and her body tense. "I can hang on," she replied. "This may be the easy part."

That made him think. His mind was unfettered and despite the fact that he could not conjure up Mark Day as an avenging angel, he could still use his reasoning power.

They had him, hog-tied and helpless, so there was no need whatever to play any games with him. If Celestine was indeed with them, they could have taken her outside and he would not know for sure after that what had happened; her cover would still not be blown. They did not need to torture her to win his sympathy and belief in her, as far as they knew that point had been won long ago. Therefore he had to consider the possibility that she belonged to some other faction, one not working with their captors.

The Russians and the Chinese were at each other's throats, therefore their respective agents, native and recruited from other sources, would be opponents. There were also other adverse powers to be considered; she could well belong to one of them.

Smith's promised cover would be useful, damn useful, but he had slipped it with the train ride; no tags however skilled could have kept them in sight and they were the only guests at the hotel. It was possible that the cover people would catch up, but would they know where to look?

They might, the hotel could tell where they had gone. But the car had not returned. It was unlikely that the hotel people would have put him into a car driven by strangers; in a city the size of tiny Darjeeling they would know everyone in the tourist business. Somehow, therefore, the driver and guide had been persuaded that their services were no longer wanted. The tall man had not bothered to tell them that their car was not returning; it would have done him no good to inform them and he was not one to waste an unnecessary word.

It added up to no cover, no returning car, almost no chance whatever that anyone would come by to rescue them before their captors returned. The most likely time would be early evening — darkness was the greatest coverall there was for things and happenings that outsiders were not supposed to see. That meant an entire long day wired to the chairs with the physical discomfort automatically mounting relentlessly minute by minute.

"Are you as helpless as I am?" he asked.

"Yes." She was trying to move her body as little as possible.

190

"We may get some help," he offered.

"I don't think so."

"My fault," he admitted. "I was damned careless, and I let you in for this."

"No, I wanted you to take me with you."

How many women were there, he asked himself, who in frustrating, agony-filled circumstances like that, could resist the temptation to blame someone else for their misfortune and humiliation — to vent their justified rage on something or somebody? That was another proof that she was a professional, but what a helluva good one! Until he had looked away from the overpowering mountain and had seen the man with the dead face and the gun.

"I don't know what's going to happen now," he said, "It may be very rough, but it's almost worth it to me — after last night."

She looked at him and somehow she managed to compose her features and regain her dignity. "When this is all over, I think we should go back to where we were." Her voice was smooth and even, not a crack showed anywhere.

"You are the greatest thing that ever happened to me," he told her. "Not because you stepped right out of the pages of my books. I thought about you, dreamed about you, and pictured you every way that I could. Now I know you, and you exceed them all."

"I belong to Mark Day," Celestine said. "I have a man I can utterly believe in, and trust. You are Mark Day, whether you know it or not, but you've added so much more."

"I wish you didn't have a dime," he told her, "so that I could go after you and you'd know it was for yourself alone. I mean that."

Celestine leaned forward, despite the fact that it had to cause her added pain in her pinioned wrists. "I do know that," she declared. "I've known it since the first day we met in the hotel lobby in Vienna. "I've known you a long time, because I've read every word you've published and your footprints are on every page."

"I want you," he said simply.

"All right," she answered.

He remembered then that he had forgotten to count one asset — time. If he could make it work for them, instead of against them, the difference could be tremendous. His heart was pounding, but he could no longer afford to think about that. He sat very still, his physical senses dulled, while he applied his brain with close to total concentration to the problem at hand. He knew that they were wanted alive, and that in itself was a great asset; it was almost binding insurance against retaliation if he could manage anything at all.

He studied with close concentration every detail of the small room they were in, then all that he could see about the construction of the chair to which he was wired. Everything that was visible he evaluated as a possible aid or weapon. Then he contemplated the possibility of some-how maneuvering himself back to back with Celestine so that with his fingers he could undo the wires that held her or vice versa, but her chair was far heavier than his and such an attempt was foredoomed by the position in which she had been placed.

When he had thought as far as he could, he remembered the lessons he had been taught by the Japanese masters who had made him proficient in karate. A great part of that lethal art was mental, including the ability to lock out

192

external factors when in an intense combat situation. His wrists were beginning to pain him severely, but he could not yield to that; the agony would probably become far more severe before long and even worse after that. In the true spirit of mind control he consciously let his *ki* flow and determined to ignore that unavoidable inconvenience. He only hoped that the man who had bound him had been a little more considerate of Celestine; the real pain was in thinking of her in agony too.

He tested carefully how far he could lean forward. He was able to manage more than forty-five degrees at the expense of stabbing bursts of torture from the ruthlessly tight wires. His feet were still on the floor; he found that by pressing down with his toes he could raise himself slightly.

First he rehearsed very carefully in his mind exactly what he intended to do, making sure that he had the pattern firmly fixed and would be able to carry it through no matter what he had to endure in the process. That done he gathered his determination, adjusted his breathing, and froze out of his brain any admission of the pain he was feeling or of the added intensity he could expect. Fully ready and in entire command of himself, he rocked slightly backwards, then forward with greater force and succeeded in getting all of his weight onto the balls of his feet. He was awkwardly bent over and blood began to paint his fingers, but for the moment he had his balance.

With his teeth set and his mind rigidly focused entirely on the thing he was attempting, he shifted his weight sideways and thereby advanced his left foot a good eight inches. As soon as he had reclaimed his balance he swung the other way and gained another eight inches forward.

A total of sixteen such excruciating maneuvers brought him directly in front of the door. There he bent down as far as he could at a cruel cost in pain he could not block out and took the doorknob into his mouth. He closed his teeth on it, feeling for a firm grip, and then tipped his head to turn it. On the fourth try he was able to release the latch and pull the door inward enough to keep it from reseating itself.

That accomplished, he twisted back to give himself room, then turned himself in his doubled-over, totally awkward position to where the numb fingers of his right hand were against the jamb. He commanded them to move. At first they refused, but by putting out the maximum amount of determination he could muster, he forced them to respond. In that way he pried the door open and then gave it a final push to make it swing wide. With that triumph it seemed to him as though he was actually conquering the pain that almost made him dizzy. He had to go on or else everything he had endured up to that point would be wasted. With that one idea locked in the forefront of his mind, he worked his way through the doorway. It was unexpectedly difficult. First, his leg muscles were beginning to protest violently against the distorted position they had been holding so long. Then, in a moment of carelessness, he had allowed the chair to hit against the doorframe, and the resulting pain in his wrists almost made him lose consciousness. The cold fresh air outside helped; he allowed himself to sink back on the chair and to rest for a few moments while he replanned once more from his new vantage point.

Praise be to God, he had remembered almost the exact size and shape of the doorstep. As he rested and eased his breathing, he re-evaluated what he intended to do and once more measured the chance he had to take. When he had finished he rocked himself to his feet once more and was ready.

He turned himself around in one minute of shooting pain, then backed up until he was positioned forty-five degrees across the corner of the two-foot-by-four-foot block of concrete that served for a doorstep. He composed himself for a moment, asked God for help, took a deep breath, and then by flexing the balls of his feet sprang backward over the edge. The instant he was airborne he threw himself forward as much as he could.

He had known that he would have only one try, and he made it count; as he came down, the horizontal brace of the chair that connected the two front legs caught on the projecting corner of the concrete, strained, and snapped. He had tried to lean forward far enough so that he would not be thrown onto his back, but he failed in that; as the rung caught the concrete with the full force of his weight, the impact was too much to counteract and he was thrown over backward hard against the ground.

He lay completely still for almost a full minute while he tried to assess his physical condition and what he had accomplished. The pain in both his wrists and his ankles was more severe still, but he was beginning to accept it as inevitable and he did not allow it to interfere with his mental processes.

His legs were wired to the outside of the chair; that meant that he could press inward against the chair structure without putting any more strain on his already lacerated flesh. He tried first with his right leg, putting as much sudden force as he could manage and thought that he detected a very slight result. The next time he tried it with both legs, attempting to scissor them together. It was barely possible that the right side of the chair leg was loosening. Determining to ignore every other thing on the face of the earth but the effort he was making, he stared up into the high sky and every few seconds jerked his leg muscles with all the strength he could command. To divert himself from other things, he counted. On the twenty-sixth try he definitely detected that the chair leg on the left side was yielding slightly.

Drawing fresh breath through his clenched teeth he made a supreme try; he not only felt the result, he definitely heard the sound of a weakening joint. At the thirty-ninth spasm it finally let go and broke completely loose from the still-solid seat. That was enormous progress. With his suddenly freed leg Nesbitt kicked with furious energy against the remaining right chair leg and missed. The force of his blow caught his right leg just above the wires and he mercifully passed out.

When he came to there was a great deal more blood and intense burning pain, but also the hope of respite. He kicked again, a little less violently and with more careful aim. He succeeded, there was a definite sound of yielding wood. With the area between the ball of his left foot and the heel he hammered a series of short sharp blows. He no longer bothered to count, so he did not know how many it took to break the chair leg loose, but it was only a limited number. Then his feet were free. The savage wires were still cutting sharply into his flesh, and the splintered chair legs were still bound tightly to his ankles, but he could move with much greater freedom.

With the front chair legs gone, he doubled his legs as

closely under his chin as he could and then snapped downward against the chair seat. He still lay on his back which made that relatively easy. With the far greater leverage he could now command it was almost a simple matter. The chair seat resisted a half dozen of his jackknives and then broke cleanly away.

For another minute and a half Nesbitt lay still collecting himself, then the urgent demands upon him forced his stunned body into action. Almost naturally he got to his feet, walked a little unsteadily three paces to the concrete block outside the door of the summit house and then sat down. The back of the chair was still obstinately intact, but he would be able to deal with that shortly. He doubled his right leg up until the fingers of his right hand could reach the end of the wires. It hurt abominably as he tried to untwist them; each attempt swelled the tendons of his wrist and allowed the wires to bite in deeper, but nothing could dissuade him then; he kept at it until he finished. Then he endured the final agony of peeling the turns of wire that remained from the cuts they had worked in his skin.

When that was done he kicked his totally free leg a half-dozen times to restart the circulation in his foot, then set to work to free his left leg in the same way. It went slightly faster, perhaps because he had acquired a slight technique and a better ability to ignore the resulting pain. Within two minutes he stood up, straight and at his full height for the first time, and able to walk freely. With complete determination not to let anything stop him, such as some additional agony in his severely tortured wrists, he strode to the corner of the building and, swinging his shoulders to do so, he smashed the back of the chair loose against the solid concrete wall. It hurt, God how it hurt, but he held his mental block intact and kept much of it from his frontal consciousness.

Five or six blows did it and the back of the chair was in fragments. For the first time he could bring his hands together; the rest was endurable because it was so close to the end. When he had finally finished he climbed the two steps up to the doorway, saw red swimming before his eyes, and almost went out again. Sheer willpower kept him going. Close to shock, but still on his feet and conscious, he staggered into the building. He looked up, saw Celestine, and was able to speak. "I'll be right with you," he said.

———

By the time he had her free, the beginnings of a further plan of action were stirring in his mind. While he was carefully untwisting and unwinding the wire so as to cause her as little pain as possible, he considered all of the possibilities he could think of and discarded many of them as totally impractical. That included trying to flee together through entirely strange mountainous terrain; it was at least eight miles back to Darjeeling and the sanctuary of the Mount Everest. While thoughts of tetanus were in his mind, he still knew that the odds were hopeless against ruthless armed pursuit which could begin at any time.

Similarly, he did not like the idea of going down the jeep road to the main highway. They might be able to stop someone, but in that delicately balanced part of the world, the question was who — one mistake would be enough to total them out completely. Also there was an almost impassable language barrier. Added to those risks was the good chance that their captors would meet them on their way back at any moment.

He still could not understand how the Land Rover and its crew that had brought them to Tiger Hill had been persuaded to leave them there; it was remotely possible that it might come back, especially when their absence from the hotel would become a matter of concern. Since they were the only guests, it was certain to be noticed. If there was a police department in Darjeeling, they might well be called upon to look into the matter.

Those were possibilities. Meanwhile, as he carefully removed the last of the wire from Celestine's right leg, he considered how he was going to take two armed men and their commander. They were all deadly, experienced professionals, against them he had a possible element of surprise and an indefinite period of time, long or possibly very short, in which to prepare himself.

"I think that does it," he said. He saw how cruelly the wire had cut into Celestine's flesh and he could not bring himself to believe that she was one of theirs. They would not expect he would be in any position to give their work on her a close inspection and therefore they could have been far more gentle. She might even bear permanent scars and that, to him, was a bitter shame.

For a few moments Celestine continued to sit perfectly still, then she began to move her limbs as he had done, to restore the lost circulation. She did not utter even a whimper, she only continued to move until she was able to stand up in reasonable possession of herself. Then she looked at Nesbitt. "Thank you," she said. "No one else could have done it. Not even Mark Day."

"Oh yes, he could," Nesbitt answered.

"How much time have we got?" she asked.

"I don't know, I can't even guess. But I have things to do."

"Of course. Waste one minute: kiss me first."

He did and it was the balm of Gilead; how she could generate that kind of fire in him he did not know, but no one else had ever come close. When it was over she looked at him and asked, "What shall we do now?"

"I've got some things planned," he said. "I'm going outside; in the meanwhile, gather up all of the wire and straighten it out the best you can."

It still hurt him to move, but it was so much better than it had been, he did not even mind. Without even bothering to drink in again the spectacle of the high Himalaya that still was visible, he rapidly collected all of the pieces of the smashed chair and the sections of wire with which he had been bound. The wood he took behind the building and concealed underneath a small cluster of debris. Two pieces he saved: rungs that were round, hard, and moderately long. One of them had split in a way that left a long raw taper and a wickedly sharp point — he might well find a good use for that. With his two pieces of wood and all of the wire, he returned to the small building and shut the door behind him.

"While I'm working," he directed, "you can help me by keeping a sharp lookout. Tell me the first moment that you suspect anything at all."

"I will," Celestine promised.

"Another thing, if you see anyone coming, go at once back to the chair you were in and take the same position, no matter who it is. Try to suggest that you are still helpless."

"That's the easy part," she told him. "I'll keep watching. You want the door to stay shut, don't you?"

"Yes, that's right. Otherwise it would be a giveaway from a distance and we'd never have a chance."

Celestine was already carefully looking out of the window and she did not turn her head as she spoke. "If you can, get one of them. That will be enough and all we can hope for, but make them pay."

"I'll try," he promised.

He began by selecting a length of the wire that was generously coated with his own blood and straightening it out to its maximum length. He did the same with a second piece, and then twisted them together as neatly as he could with his bare hands. He added a third piece in the same way and when he was through, he had a continuous length of a little more than twelve feet. The splices he had made were Western Union type and would hold a considerable strain before yielding.

From the few pieces of available furniture he selected the two heaviest and set them close to the side walls four feet in from the door. He allowed just enough room for the door to open and then, on his hands and knees, fastened the wire five inches above the floor to one of the chair legs. He stretched the wire as tight as he could and then twisted the loose end around the bottom of the other chair he had placed. The wire sagged slightly, he had not been able to pull it quite tight enough in his bent-over position; he corrected that by moving one of the chairs a bit closer and then turning it until the wire was as tight as the chairs could be expected to hold it.

"Watch out for that now," he cautioned. "I know that

sounds unnecessary, but if you see something you might get excited for a moment."

"I understand — and I won't."

The sound of her voice was a comfort to him as he went to the front window and verified for himself that no one was in sight. That done, he went outside and searched among the stones on the hilltop until he found two that suited him; he put them on the entrance block and went quickly behind the building to where he had cached the broken chair. He pawed among the pieces and then selected what he wanted. With his new possessions he hurried back inside.

Taking a fourth piece of the wire that had been used on himself he straightened it out; then, picking up two short pieces of chair rung he had recovered, he twisted the ends firmly around the middle of each one. When he had finished he tested his workmanship and was satisfied.

"It's a garrote, isn't it," Celestine said.

"Yes," he answered her. "The wire is just right for it."

"Make me one too," she invited.

"All right, if I have time. Do you know how to use it?"

"I think so, yes."

He did not dwell on the possible meaning of that remark, he had too much else to think about. There was an unused chair similar to the one to which he had been bound, he took it and placed it in the exact position its mate had been. That simple task completed, he examined more carefully the two stones he had collected. He selected one of them and then took the long rung without the point and the fifth piece of wire. Like a Twentieth-Century caveman he fastened the stone to the end of the stick, pulling each wrap as tightly as he possibly could. The stone itself was rough enough to be held in position and was close to being the ideal weight for the job it was being asked to do. The weapon, when he had it completed, was crude but potent; if he got a chance to swing it properly, it could well do the job.

When he had finished that he made another garrote for her, despite the fact that he doubted if she had the strength to use it. At least it would keep her from feeling entirely helpless. Meanwhile she had been keeping her vigil at the windows, shifting every few seconds from one to another. There was still no sign of anyone returning.

For a minute or two Nesbitt rechecked everything and satisfied himself that he could do no better. Then after a deep breath or two he turned to Celestine. "I've done the best that I can," he declared. "If things work out right, it may be of some use. But I don't know how they are coming back — how many of them or in what order."

He looked again at the tripping wire with its dangerously visible splices and then once more hefted the primitive stone mallet in his hand. "If all three of them come at the same time, that will cook us no matter what. These things only work under favorable circumstances. I'll try to get one of them for you — possibly even two, but against a man twenty feet away with a gun, I'm still helpless."

"I know," she responded. "I don't think we'll make it either. But at least let's try."

"That I'll do," he promised.

12

WHILE HE WAITED, Ed Nesbitt sat down and thought. In his mind he put himself behind his typewriter and sketched out the scene in which he was shortly to become a living actor. With the detachment that was part of his professional equipment he tried to foresee how the opposition would return and how Mark Day would handle the matter. In a way it was fantasy, but in the course of developing it, an idea or two might come.

First of all, Nesbitt reasoned that the three men would not all come back and enter the summit house together. They would believe that their captives had been successfully immobilized and would stay that way. They would expect to find Celestine and himself still ruthlessly wired to their chairs: subdued, hungry, weakened by hours of unending pain, and badly frightened. Men of that type, he knew, were noted for swollen egos and for a certain delight in forcing others to submit to their will. They would take satisfaction in the suffering they had inflicted and would be entertained if they found their victims forced to remain seated in wet clothing.

Carefully visualizing the action, he saw the men arrive in their vehicle. They would not bring it all of the way to the top of the hill; it would be too clearly silhouetted there against the sky background and they would know better than to take an unnecessary chance like that. One of the gunmen would be driving with his partner beside him and the head man in the back. The only possible variation would put the second gunman in the back also — the director would never ride up front.

All three men would then get out. One, or possibly two, would start for the summit house. The driver would remain near his vehicle; not in it because in that position he would be a sitting duck. There was a cardinal rule: opposition can surface at any time without warning, and from anywhere. Nesbitt was freshly aware of that; he had just learned the lesson again the hard way. The driver would walk a few paces away, probably to where he would have some sort of cover, and there he would light a cigarette.

So scratch the driver for the first part of the operation, but only if reasonable silence could be maintained. Let him get the least hint that all was not well and he would be in action with trigger speed.

The other gunman would come in first. There was a better than even chance he would be the one who had wired them to their chairs; he had done the job and he would want to inspect his handiwork.

Since he had already demonstrated abnormal sadistic tendencies, he would probably have matching sexual drives. He would come in thinking about Celestine, an obviously high-quality, stunningly attractive girl who would be still lashed to a chair and utterly helpless. It would be easy for him to release her numbed legs, tear off her fragile underwear, and force her submission; he would take added delight from the fact that her traveling companion, husband, or whatever would be a forced spectator impotent to do anything to stop him.

After the gunman had had a little while in which to amuse himself the head man would come in, timing his arrival so he could witness the latter part of the rape. After that it was uncertain. Probably the tall man in the coat would not demean himself by following his subordinate; he would expect to enjoy himself later on if he chose. Possibly the other gunman would be summoned to take his pleasure, but the odds were that he would remain with the vehicle — at least until he realized that something was wrong.

As far as Nesbitt could project his thinking, that would be the pattern. Therefore his own plan of action would have to be based on that hypothesis. The more he could reason and plan in advance, the less he would have to improvise against a team of highly trained, efficient, heartless professionals. He felt he could get one. Two, possibly. How things had gone by then would determine the rest.

He checked the windows himself and then went out of doors to relieve himself. The blood had congealed on his wrists and ankles so that the air no longer had free access to the raw flesh and the pain was thereby materially reduced. At the risk of being caught in the open he took an additional minute or two to exercise his body, twisting his torso and swinging his arms wide to loosen the muscles. Then he hurried back in. "I suggest that you go outside," he said to Celestine, "behind the building. If by any chance they come while you're still there, lie down and be still."

Without speaking Celestine followed his suggestion; when she returned shortly he saw how red her wrists were, how the skin was torn, and wished again that he could do something to help. Once more the idea of trying to run for it came to him and again he rejected it for the same reasons as before. Their enemies were sure to return and when they did, it would be a day of reckoning.

The long hours dragged on. Thirst became a factor in the early afternoon, but the coolness of the air seemed to relieve it somewhat. Kanchenjunga was no longer visible; clouds and fog obscured the view entirely and cut them off still further from the rest of the world. No sounds whatever came to suggest that there were any other humans on or near Tiger Hill; they were as alone as they would ever be.

Nesbitt watched the progress of the sun as he caught occasional glimpses of it through the cloud cover. He had not put his watch on for the early morning trek, so he had to judge the time as best he could. Still no one came, no other sounds of life broke their isolation.

When the sun at last stood by his estimate fifteen degrees above the horizon, he spoke to Celestine. "We've got about an hour more before it will begin to turn dark. I don't think they intend to leave us here all night because there may be some early morning sunrise viewers tomorrow. So from now on is the most probable time."

"How do you feel?" she asked.

"I'm all right. I'd like to get it over with now."

"So would I. I think we will soon."

The hour passed uneventfully; the edge of the sun touched the rim of the horizon. Nesbitt was uneasy, if he had to wait until late in the evening the darkness could defeat him; his whole plan hinged on his being able to see what he was doing. Then he heard Celestine's voice, low and quiet. "Here they come."

Nesbitt went to the window, but he was careful to stand far enough back so he could not be seen from the outside. His heart jumped when he saw that his forecast had been at least partially correct: no vehicle was in sight and only one man was visible coming toward the summit house. As he came closer Nesbitt identified him as the gunman who had tied them up. That bit of information gave him an unexpected surge of satisfaction; an all-seeing Providence was putting this man into his hands. He did not intend to waste the opportunity.

As he had planned so many times in his mind during the past hours, he took the long rung that had split with a sharp tapered point, held it tightly in his hands, and whipped it once experimentally through the air. Then stepping over the tripping wire he had rigged, he took up station behind the door.

Although he had to wait less than a minute, his nerves were screaming after the first few seconds. He tried desperately to put down his emotions and remain icy calm, but he felt as though a banshee was howling in his ear. The pain in his wrists and ankles suddenly came once more to the fore. A wave of self-doubt swept over him; he was going up against a professional gunman with a piece of wood and that was all. He made a massive effort to push that thought aside and wished fervently that his palms would stop perspiring; he needed a full and powerful grip on the stick or he was done for.

Abruptly the door swung open and the man came in. Nesbitt could not see him, but he sensed that he had paused — aware at once that the chair to which he had secured Nesbitt was empty. At that moment Ed knew that if the man turned and went back out again it would all be over — all three would be forewarned and the element of surprise would be gone forever. Why in hell hadn't he thought of that before!

He locked his fingers around his weapon with all his strength, silently drew extra air into his lungs, and hoped the hope of desperation. He heard a very short vocal sound that was more a surprised grunt than anything else; then he saw his antagonist coming into view. The man started one more step, caught the wire, tripped, and fell.

Even as he was falling the gunman tried to turn his body as his hand shot underneath his coat. In that vital second Nesbitt was on him like a tiger. As he sprang from behind the door he measured his aim in a quick instant and then smashed his weapon down with all the power he possessed. He caught his man directly on the cerebellum just at the base of the skull, but the thinness of the polished rung gave it only limited striking power and Ed knew that it was not enough.

He did not hesitate for an instant; whirling his weapon around in his hands he seized the blunt end and drove the point with focused force directly into the small of the back, three inches to the right of the spine. He was not at all sure that it would go through but it did, it went in almost as if there had been no protective clothing at all. At least five inches penetrated into the kidney region and without any expert medical knowledge Nesbitt knew that he had done the job.

He seized the man's right arm and upper right leg and with a demoniac heave half slid, half threw him into the corner behind the door. He took one quick glance through the window to see how close the next man was. He saw nobody. Granted time, he literally hurled himself onto the body, probed with his right hand under the coat, and in a few precious seconds found the gun. With it in his hand he was suddenly calmer.

"One," he declared softly as he looked toward Celestine. She was still sitting as he had told her to; on impulse he started to toss her the gun. Even at that frantic moment his brain functioned and he caught himself just in time; in three steps he carried it to her and put it into her hand. "Don't use it unless you have to," he said.

"All right." She understood at once.

"Can you?" he asked.

"Yes."

He turned quickly to take up his post once more and all but froze; the tall man was framed in the doorway. Deprived of his weapons Nesbitt flung himself forward, head down, to butt. With a reflex action that was incredibly fast the tall man jerked his right hand out of his coat pocket, raised it, and chopped hard downward for the base of Nesbitt's neck.

By the grace of God Ed sensed it coming; in the fraction of a second that he had he threw himself downward to escape the blow and his head went between his opponent's legs. The head scissors came almost instantly with crushing power; Nesbitt countered by jerking backward, using the tall man's own power to keep his head locked in. It was enough to pull the man forward off-balance, but the response was immediate. The man released his grip almost instantly, drew his body together, and rolled expertly to his feet.

His face was toward the rear wall; even before he turned he slashed a vicious back kick that would have smashed Nesbitt's face into a bloody mass if it had landed. Ed took the blow on his shoulder after most of its power had been spent, seized the ankle, and then spun his own body hard to the right. He felt the knee yield and knew that his opponent was going down again, but the tall man, even as he fell, cocked his other leg. Nesbitt dove, avoiding the kick but losing the advantage of being on his feet. He had no time to think or to remember anything he had been taught; by near instinct he jerked himself onto his side and drove his right foot with a hard leg snap toward his opponent's head.

He missed the point he aimed for, but he landed hard enough to slow his man up for a second or two; in that time he sprang to his feet, cocked his own right leg, and delivered a side-thrust kick to the abdomen with genuine authority. He did not have time to assess the exact position of his opponent, he only knew that the tall man was rising with whipcord speed and that he would have a great height advantage in less than a second. As the kick sank home Nesbitt saw that his man was momentarily doubling up;

without thought he raised his left hand into chopping position and brought it down with stinging power just under his opponent's right ear.

Some instinctive survival sense that had been willed him by his primeval ancestors told him to turn. He whirled as fast as he could and saw the third man in the doorway, saw the raised gun in his hand, and knew. In that last second he scored the tally — he had taken two of them. Then he gulped air to die.

He heard the crash of the gun and waited for the shock of the bullet. As he had written so many times, there was a moment's delay before he could feel anything, then he saw the red spurt on the front of the gunman's chest and he knew that it was Celestine who had fired.

In silent fascination he watched the man begin to slump, saw his knees unlock, and heard the sound as his gun hit the floor. There was a thud and then it was quiet. Silence, almost deadly silence, filled the summit house while Nesbitt stood still, almost unable to move. Then the intense grip of his mind over his body began to relax and he started once more to breathe. Remembering, he turned quickly once more because the man he had felled was dangerously close behind him. He looked first at the man, motionless on the floor, and then at Celestine who still sat upright in the chair, the gun held firmly in her fingers.

"Three," she said.

Nesbitt heard her and understood, but he was distracted by another sound from outside: the audible signature of a Land Rover coming the last few feet up the hill.

Almost calmly Nesbitt knelt down and took the weapon from the gunman that Celestine had shot; with it they would have a far better chance. As he moved his knees shook slightly and he had to press his hands against them to make them stop. They were still unsteady as a newcomer stepped into the doorway. He was in uniform, but on his head he wore a high turban tightly wound and tied. On its front, in the middle, was a badge that Nesbitt could not recognize or read. He did not care — he knew that this man had not come to kill them or kidnap them to some hostile territory.

"Mr. Nesbitt?" The uniformed man spoke the two words clearly and sharply; their tone and their authority lent Ed the strength he needed. He finished getting to his feet respectably well and answered, "Yes, here."

"What has happened?"

"Quite a bit. Who are you?"

"Major Singh; Indian Army."

Nesbitt drew a free and unfettered breath, the first that he had known in some time. He took hold of himself and remembered that he was a gentleman. "Good evening, Major," he said. "We're very glad to see you."

The major surveyed the interior of the room for a second time. "Are you hurt?"

"No, I'm quite all right. Miss Van Damm should see a doctor, though. Her wrists are in quite bad shape."

The major turned and called a brief order over his shoulder. In response another uniformed man appeared, coming on the double.

In deference to the Americans, the major spoke in English. "Use the radio. Pass the word that Mr. Nesbitt and his companion have been located. We will bring them in. A doctor will be needed. Order two more cars up here — immediately."

The soldier saluted smartly and hurried back to his vehicle.

Nesbitt felt that he had some explaining to do. "We came up here early this morning for the view. Our car went back for some others and did not return. Three men suddenly appeared and secured us at gunpoint; I have no idea who they are. We were left alone for several hours, then they came back and . . ." He gestured. "I'm sorry to make a mess like this," he apologized. "Also I owe you for one of your chairs."

The major delivered them back to the Mount Everest in his Land Rover with the manner of a gentleman born. He confined his conversation to the attractions of Darjeeling mountain station and suggested several things they might want to see. He recommended the Tibetan Refugee Self-Help Center where many handicraft products, including the unique Tibetan rugs, could be had. He talked about the multi-ethnic marketplace and touched on the history of the Mount Everest Hotel. As they neared their destination he also suggested that they see the Himalayan Mountaineering School which was under the direction of the celebrated sherpa Tenzing Norgay who, with Sir Edmund Hillary, had first conquered Everest. After he had expressed proper sympathy for Celestine's raw wrists, he had carefully refrained from any discussion of the events that had taken place on Tiger Hill.

At the hotel they were received warmly and with obvious relief. The manager presented himself very promptly to see what could possibly be done to make them more comfortable. The doctor had been notified and would be arriving shortly.

Nesbitt asked if dinner was by any chance still available, he had lost track of the time. Apart from that he was in good command of himself, unaware that the back of his clothing was conspicuously splattered with dried blood.

In their room he stripped down without a thought and warmed himself before the bedroom fire while Celestine was in the bathroom. He wanted to take a hot shower, but the water would be lukewarm at the best and it might well open up the still-burning cuts on his wrists and ankles. He decided that a sponge bath would do under the circumstances.

When Celestine reappeared he went inside and did the best that he could to repair some of the physical damage. He tried a wet cloth on his left wrist and found that it did more harm than good; when the doctor came, he decided, he would ask for a tetanus booster. There was no point in taking any unnecessary chances.

He came out at last, cleaner and aware that he had a pressing appetite. Celestine had already dressed, not as elaborately as before, but her hair in particular was neat and lovely.

"By the way," he said to her, "there was something I wanted to mention."

She came toward him and from a short distance away looked into his face.

"Thank you for saving my life."

"You're more than welcome," she answered. "It was a pleasure."

He studied her for a moment. "That was a very good shot, I saw where it went in."

Celestine dropped her head before she looked at him once more. "Actually, it was long overdue," she said. "I've let you down. You see, I'm the cover you were promised that you'd have."

13

WITH A MAGNIFICENT LAZINESS that had been developed through uncounted centuries of time, the waters of the Indian Ocean sent gentle rolling waves to caress the southern beaches of the verdant island of Bali. As the bright tropical sun bestowed its blessings of warmth and relaxation, a languid unhurried breeze slowly moved the tops of the myriad palm trees in a flowing pattern of contentment. Just back from the water, in command of its own sweeping cove, the luxurious Bali Beach Hotel stood in splendid isolation, an island of amenities in a setting of unrivaled beauty and peace.

From the private balcony of the seventh floor corner suite the full intoxicating perfume of the exotic island could be inhaled with every breath. Almost directly below, the huge swimming pool lay flat in the sun and shadow, reflecting the brilliance of the sky overhead. In a small cluster of palms a five-piece gamelan orchestra was effortlessly producing the liquid, bell-like flow of unbroken patterns that form the soul and substance of Indonesian music. The air was rapier clear to the point where in the far distance the outlines of snow-white clouds could be seen powdering the slopes of the mountains of Java.

From the tropically furnished sitting room of the elegant suite Gretel Hoffmeister came casually out onto the balcony, a piece of fruit in her hand. She wore a bikini so extremely minimal that her ripe figure was displayed to its fullest advantage. With nubile ease she stretched herself out on a chaise lounge, put one hand behind her head, and took another bite from the ripe mango she held.

Presently George Smith followed, bearing two inviting tall glasses. He had on a pair of white shorts that revealed his muscular legs, well-formed for a man and spoiled only by a savage scar halfway from the knee to the hip where he had once been shot. His mood was cheerful and buoyant as he handed one of the tall drinks to Gretel and then plopped into a chair with the other. He tipped his head far back and allowed himself a few moments to enjoy the respite of a well-deserved holiday.

The melodic sound of the surf and the steady polyrhythms of the gong music added to the aura of utter relaxation and contentment. Smith tried his drink and found it good, then he rolled his head to one side and allowed himself the gratification of a detailed inspection of Gretel who did not mind in the least.

When Celestine Van Damm appeared in the doorway ready to come out onto the balcony too, she provided a definite added attraction. It was possible that her bikini was a minute fraction more ample than Gretel's, but it still revealed practically all, as it had been designed to do. Apart from the flesh-colored dressings that she still wore closely taped to her ankles and wrists she, like Gretel, was as close to physical perfection as any reasonable man could ask. Her bikini top had been cunningly cut to emphasize her richly full but not overblown breasts, and it succeeded superbly. As she paused, standing up, George Smith drank his visual fill and was contented; he had little more to ask of anyone or anything at that moment.

"How is our sleeping colleague?" he inquired.

"I think we ought to call him," Celestine said. "He's missing too much of this."

With that Smith was in full agreement, but before he could speak, Gretel arose. "Let me get him," she offered.

"Why not," Celestine answered.

Gretel set down her drink and laid the remains of her mango beside it. As she walked back into the sitting room Smith had an excellent rear view of her that the tiny swatch of bikini did almost nothing to obstruct. Her movements were intensely feminine; every retreating step that she took was potent. Smith sighed and shut his eyes.

Ed Nesbitt was still buried in his pillow as Gretel came in; he was not aware of her presence or of anything else in the conscious world until she stretched herself directly beside him on the edge of the bed. Then he woke up.

He lifted his head and looked at her. "Good morning," he said. "If it's still morning, that is."

Gretel amused herself by running her fingers through his disheveled hair. "I came to get you out of bed," she announced with a caressing voice.

"You're going about it the wrong way."

She laughed lightly, then bent down and kissed his cheek. "Don't tempt me," she whispered into his ear. Then she got up and walked very casually out of the room.

After he had rubbed his hands hard over his face to bring himself into sharper focus with reality, Nesbitt sat up, gathered himself, and then swung his feet onto the floor. After he came out of the bathroom he felt measurably better. He dressed very informally in light slacks and a batik shirt he had bought in Singapore. Then he went next door to the corner suite where he first knocked and then entered without invitation.

Smith came to meet him. "We've been waiting for you," he said. "We're going to have some breakfast sent up. While we're eating it, we can talk a little."

"That sounds fine," Nesbitt answered. He was looking out toward the balcony as he spoke, taking in all that he saw.

Smith went to the phone and placed an order. Then he moved to the bar in the corner. "How about having a light eye-opener?" he asked Nesbitt. "May I make you one?"

"How light?"

"Very. It's mostly tropical fruit punch, with just a little rum."

"Heavy on the ice."

"Coming up."

Nesbitt looked around the room for a moment and then walked out onto the balcony. Celestine turned to greet him. "Come here," she said.

He obeyed. As she kissed him, he grew two inches and dropped five years. She led him to the chaise lounge and pulled him down beside her, assuming the right of possession. Nesbitt sat, then for a moment looked out at the incomparable scene before him, trying to absorb it all. He told himself still one more time that the intoxicating girl beside him was Celestine Van Damm and whatever her real name might be, no other person would ever be able to fit into that role. In a way they were an absurd pair with their matching bandages so conspicuously visible, but he cared nothing what people might think — it was none of their damn business.

Celestine took his arm and put it around her warm body. "Before anything else comes up, I want to tell you something," she said. "When I first met you, I teased you about being Mark Day. Do you remember on the terrace in Venice?"

"Of course."

"When you told me so definitely that you weren't Mark Day I was a little amused, inside." She paused for a moment. "Well, not any more. If you want the truth of it, I don't think that Day himself could have equalled what you did up on that mountain."

Ed Nesbitt was a little uncomfortable despite the enviable situation he was in. "Let me explain something to you," he began. "It has to do with authors and the characters they create. To get anywhere at all, you have to lead a sort of double life almost all of the time. As a practical matter I know perfectly well that there isn't any Mark Day; I can still remember the time that I sat down and worked out the name I was going to give him. I can remember, too, inventing the various situations he has been involved in and planning their outcome."

He stopped and allowed himself to look at her again, drawing nourishment just from seeing her. "On the other hand, no author who is any good at all ever admits to himself that his people *couldn't* exist. I'm sure that L. Frank Baum had a very clear picture of the land of Oz. And when he created the tin woodman he knew how the woodman would behave, what he would say, and how he would react to any given situation. To do that he had to put himself in the position of his readers, the youngsters he wanted to entertain, and believe in the woodman himself. He did, I know that, and partly because of it, he produced a classic."

"I can understand that," Celestine said.

"There's a better example," Nesbitt continued. He squinted his eyes a little as he studied the sun on the water and let his thoughts take shape. "Charles Dickens was writing the *Old Curiosity Shop*. When he came to the point where he had to let Little Nell die, he wandered the streets of London all night with tears streaming down his face. He could have changed his story, of course, but it wouldn't have been right and he knew it. Little Nell was as real to him as if she had been his own daughter — he lived that close to his characters. So did Victor Hugo and Cervantes. Now they are all immortals."

Celestine snuggled closer as he went on. "I don't even attempt to write like that, but I do the best that I can in my own field. So I'm very much aware of Mark and sometimes, like a kid who dreams of becoming President, I put myself in his place." He changed the tone of his voice.

"Now you understand why I was so ready to accept Celestine Van Damm when I had the incredible luck actually to meet her."

"Were you disappointed?"

"No! You have no idea of the impact you made. Incidentally, you did damn well yourself when we were up on Tiger Hill. You know that."

She looked at him. "I was supposed to do much better. I let those goons get the drop on me like a school-girl amateur. I paid for it, but it cost you so much more."

"Anyhow, it worked out all right," he said.

He paused to accept a drink from Smith who had been tactfully waiting in the background. He tasted it and found that it fitted perfectly with the panorama of sea and sky that was spread out before him. When Smith had gone, Celestine suddenly tightened her grip on his arm. "Do something for me," she asked. "Please let me stay . . . who I am."

"Of course. Otherwise I could never write another book."

She continued to hold his arm around her as though it was a piece of her personal property that someone might attempt to steal. She did not let it go, in fact, until Gretel came to tell them that breakfast was waiting.

They ate, enjoying the tropical air and the comfort of their surroundings until the last of the toast had turned cold and the butter had congealed on its surface. Then Smith suggested that they move to more comfortable chairs. When they had done so, the atmosphere underwent a change and the relaxed feeling for the moment was dissipated.

"I don't want to spoil this holiday," Smith said. "We don't get one very often and it could end at any moment. But there are some things we should talk about."

He deliberately went to the bar and refreshed his drink, then he sat down again. "There's no business in the world where you have to keep your mouth shut as much as this one, but because you, Ed, have gotten so deeply involved with us, we have to talk about some things."

He looked sharply at Nesbitt. "You must understand that not one word of this can be repeated — anywhere at any time. God help you if you even hint at it in one of your books."

"I won't," Nesbitt promised.

"From this point on you're bound just as securely as if you had signed your name to a very important document. We know you, we know a lot about you, and you are entitled to what is called an element of trust. That's all, I can't go any farther."

Nesbitt nodded and kept his mouth shut.

"All right. I'll start off by telling you that every year hundreds of people write to various branches of the government offering their services as secret agents. That's their terminology — not ours. We answer all of them, politely of course, and in most cases the thank-you letter ends the matter. In some cases we take at least one look at the writer if he offers a special capability or is otherwise interesting for a particular reason. When that happens we open a file; we did with you."

"I'm honored," Ed said.

"We have an instinctive fear of journalists of any kind, because their basic discipline is to tell everything they know. In your case we found some evidence of discretion and certain other things that looked favorable, so we ran a complete check on you. It took time and cost money. If we hadn't done that, you would have been sidetracked a long time ago."

Smith waited to see if Nesbitt had anything to say, and was glad that he didn't.

"The last thing that I will ever do, God help me, is blow an agent, but since you now know that your Celestine Van Damm has certain official connections, there's no point in trying to be coy about it. But if you have any regard for her at all, you know absolutely what you must do."

"I've been doing it," Nesbitt told him. "I've known for some time."

"How?"

"You finish first."

"Very well. As part of our investigation of you, all of your books were read very carefully. It was obvious that you knew quite a lot about the trade. Now just about the time that you were planning your around-the-world trip to see publishers and soak up backgrounds, we were having some problems because of a small, but very efficient, organization of money men. Are you familiar with that term?"

"Agents who work independently, for anyone, for hire."

"That's right. We didn't know then who had employed them or what they were after, but they were causing us a good deal of trouble. That's all you need to know, apart from the fact that this kind of undercover warfare is continuous, irregardless of cease fires and summit meetings; there is literally never a time when we don't have a half-dozen jobs at least on our hands. And heaven help us if we ever let up on our vigil, because then we'll be clobbered for sure."

"I did a book on that subject," Nesbitt said.

"I know; I read it. Now about yourself. Since you're published all over the world, despite the fact that they don't have much time for enjoying fiction, a good many of the pros know who you are. They also know that you have a lot of knowledge about the business and from that they may have drawn some conclusions. This is only a guess, but some of them could have suspected that you were operating yourself. You certainly would have an impeccable cover. This could explain why a known agent was going through your luggage in Berlin."

Ed nodded. "I figured it out more or less the same way myself. I was scheduled to go to many different places and I asked a lot of questions."

"Then you can guess the next part: when we heard about your little adventure at the Schweitzerhof we broke out your file in a hurry. We had two very good reasons to stick pretty close — your own protection, at least until we were sure who you were, and also the chance to keep certain people in view. We always like to know where they are and what they're doing."

He was interrupted when a smiling waiter, complete with a flower behind his ear, came to remove the breakfast table. As soon as the man had left, Smith continued. "We learned very quickly that the attaché case you were carrying was identical to some special ones of our own. That was a clear break for us, so we sicked Gretel onto you — we may as well call her that — and made the switch. Unfortunately, you caught onto it almost immediately. So we reached into the bag and produced Miss Celestine Van Damm for you."

Nesbitt raised his hand. "May I be allowed to guess for a moment or two?"

"Please do, I'd like to know how you have it figured out." He was seconded by Gretel Hoffmeister who nodded her head as she looked at him.

Nesbitt took hold of Celestine's hand without realizing that he had done so. "I started Mark Day about nine years ago after reading up extensively on espionage and its related fields. When the first book was successful and my publishers wanted another, I felt that Mark should have a steady girl friend. So I put some pieces together that seemed to fit and then deliberately picked a name for her that was possible, but very unlikely. It worked, and I kept her in the series. But it was all on paper until, without any warning whatsoever, I found a man going through my bags in Berlin."

"At which point you proceeded to take him bare-handed within a few seconds," Smith interjected. "It couldn't have been more than that."

For a moment Nesbitt's mind was thinking so literally he spoke automatically. "No, Mark Day did that."

For just a moment Smith sat perfectly still, looking straight ahead and seeing nothing. His teeth were together as he thought. "Wait a minute. Now I think I understand. I couldn't see how you could possibly have psyched yourself so high so fast. You shifted gears, Ed Nesbitt to Mark Day!"

Nesbitt cursed himself for having opened his mouth without thinking first, but there was no way he could deny what he had just said. "You could put it that way if you want to," he admitted.

"And in the bazaar in Istanbul?"

"Yes."

"Ed," Smith said, "I wish to hell I could do it."

That took the sting out of what had been almost a childish admission. Nesbitt stole a quick glance at Celestine and saw that she was smiling encouragement at him. He felt better after that; if she approved of him, that was all he required.

He decided to go on. "For a while I assumed that I had surprised an ordinary hotel sneak thief. I don't believe that that kind usually carries steel, but it was the most probable answer until I ran into Gretel. That changed things; at that point I knew that I was involved in something, but I had no idea what. Since I knew that the case I had been handed wasn't my own, the best answer that I could come up with then was that I was being used as a dummy, or an unwitting courier. I understand that that is relatively common."

"That's true," Smith agreed.

"I held onto that idea until I met Celestine," Nesbitt continued, "then everything turned around once more. I believe in coincidences, but having my own creation suddenly turn up in person was incredible. I *might* have swallowed it, because I really wanted to, but when she appeared just after two other very unusual things had happened to me, I simply had to know better. So I thought about it. She fitted the part perfectly, there was no denying that, and the story she told sounded believable. It was a magnificent piece of bait, but there were two realistic questions that wouldn't go away: what was her real identity, and whom was she working for?"

Smith leaned back for a moment and looked at the ceiling. "We reasoned that if you got the word that Miss

228

Celestine Van Damm was in the lobby asking for you, it would be pretty likely that you would at least want to take a look at her."

"I'd have walked over red-hot coals," Nesbitt said. "And after I did look at her, I wanted her to be Celestine Van Damm so badly I could taste it. But it was plainly impossible. I pretended to go along with the story she was telling me, but I was thinking awfully damn hard. She could have been just a girl who fancied herself in the part and who had decided to have a go at it just for fun. The timing argued against that. Secondly, she could have been one of your people, George, but I couldn't come up with any good reason at the time why you would have put her in. It was right there under my nose, but I missed it. Lastly, she could have been working for the opposition."

Celestine herself spoke. "We did meet once briefly quite a while ago; I told you the truth about that."

Smith carried on for her. "You had us just a little worried long before the Berlin incident, Ed, because your fictitious Celestine was uncomfortably close to an actual girl we knew very well. She had the same general background: a genuine jet setter with lots of money and all that. But she also had brains and a desire to do something more than just float around as an expensive ornament. Since she was doing a lot of traveling into some interesting areas, we contacted her and asked if she would care to help us out now and then. Nothing dangerous, just more or less keep her ear to the ground and let us know the results whenever we asked. Fortunately for us, she was willing. We used her sparingly, but when we did, she produced."

He looked at Celestine, who picked up the ball. "Something else that I told you was true — a lot of the people that I know read your books and were certain that I was the girl in them. When they asked me if I had ever met you and I said 'yes,' that clinched it. Believe it or not, I was even invited once to visit an archeological meeting."

Smith continued. "When you gave your performance in Berlin, it was so good we were immediately suspicious — perhaps we had missed something. While we were deciding exactly what to do, someone came up with the bright idea that we produce Celestine Van Damm in person and see how you would react to that. After you came to the embassy in Vienna and told us that you were on to the attaché case switch, we decided to put her in to get a further reading on you."

"She succeeded," Nesbitt said.

Smith chose to ignore that. "We had you covered in Prague even though that's a difficult area. We were with you that evening when you went for a walk. When we learned that you had a tag, and knew who was responsible, we re-evaluated the situation once more. Celestine herself suggested that she be assigned as additional cover. We talked that over and agreed."

Celestine kicked her bare foot a few inches into the air. "I talked him into it," she declared. "He didn't want to trust a mere female that hadn't been properly schooled." She looked at Nesbitt. "I wanted the job," she added.

Smith grimaced. "We had a tip, never mind how, that an attempt was going to be made to snatch your case in Venice, so we put Celestine in to cover it. She was definitely expecting something, you understand, so when the snatch was made, she was prepared. She got the ID of the boat and passed it on when she made the phone call. That helped a lot in getting the case back so quickly." Smith spent a moment with his drink and then deliberately became more casual. "Whatever else she may have decided to do was her own affair and her own idea. Not in the line of duty, in other words."

Nesbitt started to say something and then thought better of it.

"It was my own carelessness that allowed you to get a look at me in Istanbul," Smith continued. "I knew perfectly well that you were coming in early, but I had you pegged at a different hotel. I didn't check and that's my fault. Then came your astonishing performance in the Grand Bazaar; right then and there I refused to believe any longer that you weren't an agent and an extraordinarily capable one. I bought the same idea that our competitors had, and as for them, you must have erased their last possible doubt. I turned Washington upside down trying to find out who you really were and whom you were working for. I ended up believing that some of the best and most reliable friends that I have were lying to me."

Gretel Hoffmeister stretched her arms forward as she sat in her chair. "It was a dilly," she said.

"I'm really sorry I caused you so much trouble," Nesbitt apologized.

"You needn't be," Smith told him. "During our little chat in Bombay you answered some questions for me. You told me your deduction about the radio in the attaché case, and of course you were right. But I still couldn't determine to my own satisfaction whether you were working along with us or were a very cool customer from across the railroad tracks."

"So you sent for Celestine once more."

"Technically she volunteered, not that we gave her

much choice. When you headed up to Darjeeling we were worried about her — it was much too close to unfriendly borders, and there was no good way we could provide backup cover under the circumstances. Our justification was that we had to know what was going on and calculated risks are part of the business."

Smith stopped, letting the cobwebs of conflicting thoughts clear out of his brain. There was a hint of relief in his voice when he went on. "What happened up on Tiger Hill answered all of our questions. The principal money man grabbed you. Then he made a fairly fast trip to a point not far from Darjeeling where he made a deal."

"What kind of a deal?" Nesbitt asked.

"He sold you. And for quite a good fee, too. He agreed to deliver both of you alive and well for interrogation, and you know the professional meaning of that word."

Nesbitt looked at him carefully. "How did you learn that?" he asked.

Smith actually smiled. "We don't need to go into that. Sufficient to say we know now where you stand. Incidentally, you made a rather good impression on the lady to your immediate right, and that is certainly worth something. Now that I've had my say, I want to know just how you managed to spot her."

Nesbitt took his time; he actually seemed to be embarrassed. "She did very well in Vienna," he began. "She very nearly sold me an impossible story, one I would have liked to have believed. But, as I told you, having her turn up like that just after two other extraordinary events in the same week was too much to swallow."

He showed signs of wanting to stop, but a look at Smith told him that he had no choice.

"Well, when we first met in Venice, and you would normally expect that she would be full of bright chatter, she asked me almost immediately about my case and wanted to know what was in it. That was out of character; young women aren't usually interested in the contents of business briefcases, especially not in a romantic setting at the foot of the Grand Canal.

"Secondly, she knew in advance which room I was going to be assigned. When I asked her where she was, she answered, 'I'm right next to you, didn't you know?' It couldn't have been a coincidence, because as soon as I arrived at the hotel and checked in I was told that she was waiting for me on the terrace. So they had us tabbed as being together and I didn't tell them. Either she had set it up herself or someone had done it for her."

"Anything else?" Smith asked.

"When we were talking in Bombay you contradicted yourself while we were discussing her. First you told me that you had had me thoroughly checked out. Then when Celestine came up and I told you that I thought that she was one of your people, you said something like, 'Absolutely not; I assumed that she was your regular girl friend you've been writing into your books.' If you had checked me out as you said, you couldn't possibly have missed a regular girl friend."

"*Touché,*" Smith admitted.

"Another thing: you asked me to tell you all about her. You had to know already, if you were covering me as you said you were. And the cover was there, I knew that, because you were aware of the balcony dodge I used in Prague. You mentioned it yourself."

233

Smith found solace in his drink. "What else did you get?" he asked.

"Celestine knew altogether too much about my travel plans. The only people who had copies of my itinerary were yourself and my travel agent, yet she showed up in Calcutta right on schedule. That's what told me that she most likely was not with the opposition. Up until then I had thought that she was."

"Why?" Gretel asked.

"Because in Venice she suggested that we walk along the canals and that was where the case was grabbed. I would never have gone there on my own."

Smith was calm. "I expect that you have more," he said.

"Not really. But up on Tiger Hill, while we were being wired to those chairs, it was all that I could do to keep from exploding verbally; I only shut up because I knew it would give added pleasure to the men who had me helpless. When it was her turn, Celestine sat there like a stoic and let them tie her down without a word. Considering my own discomfort, I thought it was remarkable that she was able to control herself that well. I wondered how many women in the world would be able to submit to that, even at the point of a gun, without saying *something*. But a pro would. Not conclusive, but it reinforced what I already knew."

That was enough and he knew it. Nesbitt got up and then looked down at Celestine. "I'm sorry," he said.

Smith rose as well. "Ed," he declared. "It's just possible that we may accept your offer, as per your original letter. It's on file, and I can arrange matters."

"Could we talk about that later?" Nesbitt asked.

"We can. Now you're going to have to excuse us; I'm going to take Gretel up to meet Blanco, the artist. He lives here on Bali, you know. I want to see if he can be persuaded to paint her."

"Good luck. I know about him, I've seen some of his work in museums. One of the very greatest for nudes, I understand."

"Come to think of it, I believe you're right."

"I'll change," Gretel said.

"Don't wear anything tight," Smith advised her. "It could leave marks."

Ten minutes later they had left. The somewhat painful talk was over, the events of the past several weeks seemed to have reached their climax and disappeared, but Nesbitt's thoughts were still restless. He wandered out onto the balcony, took hold of the railing, and looked out as far as he could across the water. It seemed to him that he did not know who he was. His mind gave him a clear and factual answer; he was Edwin Nesbitt, novelist, who had had some success in the popular field. He would soon have to go home and start on a new book.

But here he was, thousands of miles from his home and workroom, standing in the light of the Indonesian sun at one of the most exotic and fabulous locations the world held in its storehouse. And he knew that for just a little while he had indeed stepped into the dark and secret world of espionage and had played an actual living role on that stage. Here in the bright light of day, feasting on the tropical splendor of this jewel island in the Southern Hemisphere, the harsh cruelties he had undergone on that now-distant mountaintop at the border of India, and the pain that he had endured, were over and done with. Now he could only go back to the mundane, and that would be a very hard thing to do.

He was aware when Celestine came up behind him despite the fact that she made almost no sound. He felt her presence and his imagination supplied the warmth of her body. "Please forgive me," he said without looking around. "I didn't want to make you look bad, and I realize that I did. I tried to fix it by throwing in that bit about Smith himself, but it didn't help very much."

He felt her then, and heard her voice as she spoke from behind his right shoulder. "Oh yes, it did. Now I've got a good one on him. He won't say anything — he won't dare."

"I like him," Nesbitt commented. "Not my idea of an agent at all."

"He isn't an agent really, he's more a director — a higher-up. He has a lot to say about what goes on."

"Gretel seems to like him."

"She does."

He caught the slight change in her tone. "He's married, I take it."

"Yes." She left it simply at that. She could have added a comment, but she knew better.

"He's entitled to a holiday," Ed said.

"Yes, he is."

That settled that.

Celestine moved to the chaise lounge and sat down. Then she looked up and silently expressed a wish. Ed obeyed and sat beside her.

"I want to ask something of you," she said. "Something very important."

Nesbitt was almost afraid of what it might be. "All right," he answered, "What can I do for you?"

"You heard a lot about me this morning and it's all quite true. Things concerning my background, the kind of person I am, even the invitation to attend the archeological meeting. Do you believe me?"

"Yes, I do."

"When we first met, in Vienna, I told you that my name, my real name, wasn't too far from the one you used in your books."

"I remember that," Nesbitt said. "But I don't want to know what it is. Don't ever tell me."

"I don't intend to. Now the big thing I want to ask: it's an awful lot, so think before you answer. Will you allow me to change my name, legally, to Celestine Van Damm? It would mean usurping something that's your property, and valuable."

Ed turned until he was no longer facing the water and the panoramic spectacle of beach, palm trees, islands, and mountains. He looked instead at the young woman who was close beside him. "Are you sure that you want to take a step like that?" he asked.

"Yes," she answered him. "I want to very much."

"If you do, may I still write about you in my books?"

She seemed almost hurt. "Certainly, what do you think! Just one thing: don't ever believe, not for one moment, that I want to do this for publicity."

"I know better than that. Actually I'm very deeply honored. More than you know."

"Thank you."

There was almost a half a minute of silence before Nes-

bitt spoke once more. "Of course if you go and marry someone, then the deal is off. You can't very well be Celestine
Van Damm and Mrs. Elmer Titwiller at the same time."

"Of course not," she agreed. "Besides, if I get married,
Mark Day would be furious. And he's not a man to trifle
with."

"Definitely not — you'd better stay single for a while at
least."

"I intend to. But I also intend to be seen with you quite
frequently under scandalous circumstances. Can you endure that?"

"Certainly, providing that the scandal is absolutely
true."

Below them the gentle surf provided its continuous per-
cussion behind the gamelan orchestra which had begun
to play once more.

Celestine rose and almost silently disappeared through
the doorway. She had a right to go, but to Edwin Nesbitt
at that moment it felt as though a pound of his flesh had
been cut away. He took a hard grip and determined to
bring himself back down to where he rightfully belonged.
He had been riding on a cloud of enchantment; it would
be best to get off while he still could without taking a
disastrous fall.

Through the open window directly behind him he heard
her voice speaking to him. "Was that true what you said —
about being able to step into Mark Day's character when
you are suddenly thrust into a violent situation?"

"Yes," he answered more or less automatically. "You
see, I have to think about him so much out of professional
necessity, I've learned to project myself into his person-

238

ality, his ways of thinking, and his patterns of action. Please don't laugh at me."

"Never."

Something in her tone conveyed a great deal more than the single word. He rose from where he was sitting and stepped back into the living room.

There was very little change, but it was significant. He had seen her nude before, but now, in the bright daylight and in the unparalleled setting, all that he could think of was Venus on the mountaintop, waiting for Paris to give her the golden apple. She was absolute perfection as she raised her hands to smooth the hair above her ears.

"Since I'm Mark Day's girl," she said, looking at him in a way that all but burned his soul, "how about trying it now."